I couldn't let her be dead. . . .

I tried to revive Callie. I tried. I performed CPR upon her. Pound, pound, pound, pound upon her chest, then fill her lungs with my own strangled breath. No pulse. Pound, pound, pound, breathe. Pound, pound, breathe. Pound. Breathe. Pound. No pulse.

No pulse.

Sound came back to me. There was a scream. I was screaming. Callie was not dead, she couldn't be, she couldn't be, I couldn't let her be.

No pulse.

No pulse.

I rose. Inside the trunk of the car was a box I'd picked up from my lab that afternoon. In the box was a syringe and an insulated canister. In the canister was a vial. In the vial was a fluid.

I opened the trunk. I removed the box. I opened the canister. I inserted the syringe into the vial. I filled the syringe.

No pulse. I couldn't let her be dead.

I injected Callie with the reanimating solution.

Read these terrifying thrillers
from HarperPaperbacks!

Babysitter's Nightmare
Sweet Dreams
Sweetheart
Teen Idol
Running Scared
by Kate Daniel

And look for

Class Trip
by Bebe Faas Rice

The Nightmare Inn series
#1 *Nightmare Inn*
#2 *Room 13*
#3 *The Pool*
#4 *The Attic*
by T. S. Rue

FOREVER YOURS

DAVID PIERCE

HarperPaperbacks
A Division of HarperCollins*Publishers*

This is a work of fiction. The characters, incidents, and dialogues are products of the author's imagination and are not to be construed as real. Any resemblance to actual events or persons, living or dead, is entirely coincidental.

HarperPaperbacks *A Division of* HarperCollins*Publishers*
10 East 53rd Street, New York, N.Y. 10022

Produced by Daniel Weiss Associates, Inc., 33 West 17th Street, New York, New York 10011.

First printing: January, 1994

Printed in the United States of America

HarperPaperbacks and colophon are trademarks of HarperCollins*Publishers*

10 9 8 7 6 5 4 3 2 1

For Fidel and Rufus,
arrectis auribus, nolens volens.

Prologue

I can see the end of the corridor. There's a barred window where light comes in and settles into a puddle of yellow on the concrete floor. Today the puddle is bright—that means it's sunny outside. Here on the inside, though, the weather is the same every day—damp and gray.

Every day the same smells, too. Prison never changes. It always stinks of sweat and the pine-lemon cleanser they slosh everywhere. Every now and then I get a strong whiff of a guard's Old Spice or Brut. The guards make sure they don't smell too much like us, the prisoners.

I've gotten used to the sounds. It's like when you go on vacation and the crickets keep you up all night, and then after a while you don't notice them anymore. Now I hardly hear the sounds of men snoring and coughing and grunting and belching. The noises the two hundred guys in my cell block make as they shuffle restlessly around their calls. You get used to it.

You can get used to just about anything, I've learned.

My own cell isn't bad, compared to some of the others. I have it all to myself. As another inmate once said to me, you don't know insomnia until you're locked in an eight-by-eight cell with a guy who stabbed a dozen people.

The standard-issue cot is rock hard and undersized, but not too moldy. And they repainted my three gray walls only the week before I was moved in. A new paint job! Big deal.

Apparently the warden gives us serial murderers special treatment.

As I said, it's sunny today. It couldn't not be. It's graduation day for the seniors of Ellswood High School—my former classmates. They always have the ceremony outside on the football field. If it were raining out, they would move into the auditorium. But no one can remember that ever happening.

Last year, when I was a junior, some of my

friends graduated. A stage was set up under the goalposts. The seniors sat in foldout chairs, lined up starting around the five-yard line. The crowd reached all the way back to midfield. By the time the losers with names like Wyman and Yeager were called to the stage, everyone was more than ready to throw their caps in the air and start partying.

This year graduation will be a solemn occasion, though. I've been lying on my cot, thinking about it, about how it'll be—thinking about my friends and their families getting ready this morning. I myself had a new suit—I'd been waiting for this day for almost four years.

But today there won't be any cheers. There'll be no whistles, no backslapping—only half-hearted congratulations and perhaps hugs of comfort. There won't be any jokey signs like "Made It Through Alive!" on the top of anyone's cap—that would be hitting a little too close to home. No one will do a cartwheel on stage, like Lita Young, head cheerleader, did last year.

Some of the girls will be sobbing quietly, and even the tough guys, the motorheads and jocks, will be sober. My whole class is going to be pretty somber, pretty down. In their black

3

gowns, they'll seem like they're in mourning.

There will be four empty chairs set up among the graduates. One will be at the twenty-two-yard line; one at the thirty-eight; one at the forty-three; and one around the forty-four. Four empty chairs. For the four murdered students of Ellswood High School.

I can see it now, see it as if I were there. The black gowns, the green turf, the blue sky. The awards and speeches. The white diplomas, with the gold seals shining.

And I should be there. I should be there with them, instead of pressing my forehead against a cold steel bar until the bones in my head ache. Instead of straining to catch a glimpse of the dingy sun at the end of a concrete corridor.

After all—where, among all those puffy, tear-streaked faces assembled in the football field, is the valedictorian? Where is the star pupil, the kid for whom everything was a snap, the most likely to succeed? Where is the Golden Boy?

Right here. He's right here.

He's right here.

One

"Hey, Alec, save me and Gina a place, will you?" Ian Golder called to me as he and his girlfriend picked up their lunch trays and got in line. I was standing with my tray, already heaped with nutritious-and-delicious cafeteria swill. I scanned the room for a table with three empty seats. It was that most-dreaded date, the Wednesday after Labor Day. Black Wednesday. The first day of a new school year.

Ian and I had compared our schedules when they'd come in the mail a couple of weeks earlier. Different homerooms, different English classes, different study halls. Those would have been our only chances at having class together. I was taking lots of science—bio, organic chem, physics, the whole bit. Ian was taking it easy senior year—automatic pilot, he called it. Cruise control. His day was filled with stuff like music appreciation and "History of Cinema." That meant he got credits for listening to CDs and watching videos. If Ellswood had offered basket weaving, Ian would have signed up for the intro section. We were going to be spending most of our time at opposite ends of Ellswood High. But luckily, we did get the same lunch period.

Darting over to a half-empty table, I set down my tray and spread my books in front of the two chairs across from me. Already the tables were beginning to fill up.

Within a week, the various groups and cliques would find themselves and stake out their territories. The freaks would congregate near the courtyard door, so they could duck out for a quick smoke. The jocks would assemble in a nearby corner, where they could hurl insults and french fries at the freaks and be safe from counterattack from behind. Next to them would be the cheerleaders, who pretended to be grossed out by the jocks but who couldn't take their eyes off them. The preppies and student-government types would occupy the middle of the cafeteria, where they could see and be seen by the maximum number of kids. The lepers, chess teamers, geeks, and all the freshmen—except the very prettiest girls, who would get invited to sit with the jocks—would be pushed to the farthest, darkest corner of the room, where they would dream about the day when they would take over the world or become sophomores.

I spotted Ian and Gina across the room, wandering among the tables. "Hey, Ian! Gina!" I hollered. "Over here." Ian looked over, rolled his eyes, and started toward me.

I'd known Ian since grade school. We still shuddered at the memory of old Mrs. Lowenburger, who terrorized us in third grade. Like soldiers who go through basic training together, Ian and I had formed an unbreakable bond in Mrs. Lowenburger's boot camp. We'd been best friends ever since.

"So how were your first three classes, Alec?" Gina Phelps sat down next to me. "Have you convinced your teachers to hang it up and just let you teach?" she asked.

Ian and Gina had been going out for over a year, since the summer between sophomore and junior years. She had very large, very brown eyes and an oval face. She wore her straight brown hair in a pageboy cut that was completely out of style. But you had to admit it looked great on her.

"Not yet," I said. "I'll let Buckland keep teaching bio—he needs the practice. But if Ms. Kelling says 'Okay, class? Okay? Okay?' one more time in that whiny voice of hers, I'm going to grab the chalk and start solving the stupid problems myself. I don't care if she is the best-looking teacher in school."

"You don't care, huh?" said Ian. "I seem to remember you were pretty pleased when you found out you had her for calculus."

"'Ooh, Ms. Kelling—or should I call you *Felicia*?'" Gina said, waving her arm in the air. "'I know the answer to that one! Why don't I demonstrate it to you after class? In private,'" she added. "Now I know how you get all those A's, Alec."

"Well, I'm not the kind to kiss and tell . . ." I said.

"Gimme a break, Baines," Ian said. "You'd have better luck with Gurties."

"Very funny," I said. Mr. Gurties was Ellswood's principal, and despite what the old spelling lesson asserted, the principal was *not* my pal.

8

"Not to change the subject from Alec's totally intriguing love life, guys," said Gina, "but what is this thing?" She poked at her tray with a plastic fork.

"I believe that's a hamburger," said Ian. "Of course, I can't be sure." He held up his half-eaten burger. "Mine tastes like shoe polish. What do you suppose yours is, Alec?"

I took a bite of my hamburger and chewed thoughtfully. "Boot. Size ten. Vintage 1981. A tasty piece of leather, full-bodied though not cloying, subtle yet not insincere."

Gina held up a french fry. "I think I have the laces to go with your shoe polish." She pointed the french fry at Ian's tray, then at mine. "And your boot." She popped the fry in her mouth. "Gotta go—don't want to be late for my first drama class. I hear we're going to pretend to be different animals. I'm feeling clammy already." She made a face at the food on her tray and got up to leave.

"Hey, Geen, I'll meet you at your locker after fourth period, okay?" Ian asked.

"Wouldn't miss it for the world," she said, bending over to give him a quick kiss. "See you later, Alec. Oh, and hey—go easy on the teachers, will ya?"

"Right. Catch you later," I said. Ian and I watched her return her tray, then wiggle her fingers good-bye as she walked out the door. Ian waved back.

"She's really great," I said.

"Yeah," said Ian. "She really is. You ought to get one just like her." Ian tipped back in his chair, catching his feet on the underside of the table, and folded his arms across his chest. Ian was not especially tall, but he was very stocky.

"You're telling me," I said.

"What about Lori Fordham? She's nice enough, even if she is a bit of a ditz. And she's great looking—probably be Homecoming Queen this year. Didn't you have a couple of dates with her last year?"

"I went to the Sadie Hawkins dance with her because she asked me." I shrugged. "I was so surprised, I couldn't think of a polite way to say no."

"Oh, boohoo. Boo the hoo hoo. Lori Fordham flung herself at you. I should be so lucky."

"Gina would murder you."

"True," Ian said, tipping his chair back onto all fours. "But it might be worth it." He got up to return his tray. "But seriously, there's gotta be someone at this school—besides Ms. Kelling, I mean—you could go for. Maybe a freshman who doesn't know any better."

"Please. My problem isn't getting a date. My problem is there's no one I'm interested in."

"Yeah, well. Can't help you there, buddy." Ian started toward the tray return. "Aren't you gonna get going? Fourth period is about to start."

"I know. I got a couple of minutes, though." With all this talk about finding me a girlfriend, I was beginning to feel a little down. I already had my chem book with me, and I wouldn't have to make another trip to my locker before fourth period.

"Hey, you gonna come with me and Gina out to the lake this weekend? Could be our last chance to go swimming before it gets cold."

"Maybe. I'll see how much homework I have." Ian and Gina were good about including me in on things, but I couldn't help feeling like a third wheel.

"Homework? On the first weekend of school? Alec, you're a senior now. Lighten up. You've had enough credits to graduate since you were a sophomore. Drop your advanced courses. Take Intro to MTV and five periods of study hall. Do like me: cruise control." Ian made like he was driving a convertible.

"I'll think about it."

"Right. Take it easy," Ian said, disappearing into a crowd of kids rushing out the door. The bell for the second lunch shift rang, and an equal number of kids began pushing their way into the cafeteria, grabbing tables and saving places in line. I knew I should get going. But something made me stay.

Ian was right. I did need a girlfriend, but not one like Lori Fordham. I never had trouble getting dates. Getting good grades didn't automatically condemn you as a social washout, at least at Ellswood. But somehow my relationships with girls always sort of fizzled out after three or four dates.

Why couldn't I hook up with someone I really liked?

Just then I noticed a girl peering around the cafeteria. She looked lost. There was nothing so unusual about that—all the freshmen walked around in panicked confusion for the first week of school.

But this girl looked older—probably a junior or senior. She was wearing a loose, olive-green

12

turtleneck, faded blue jeans, and brown loafers. Not the sexiest outfit of all time, but on the other hand, it did show off her body. By the way she was standing, with her feet planted solidly and her shoulders thrown back, I could tell that she knew she had a good figure.

But the thing that really caught my eye was that rather than panic at being in an unfamiliar situation, there was a slight smile on her face. She seemed to be finding the idea of her own confusion humorous, as if she were the victim of an elaborate practical joke. Even she had to admit it was clever: there was hardly an empty seat in the whole cafeteria.

I found myself walking up to her. "Excuse me. Why don't you sit down over there?" I motioned to where I'd just been sitting.

"Isn't that your chair?" she said.

"I have to be leaving soon anyway. Go ahead."

"That's awfully nice of you, but I can't do that. Look, there are two places." The girl indicated with her tray. "If we move quick, we can grab both of them." She sprang toward the empty chairs before I could object.

Shaking my head, I went back to where I'd been sitting and collected my books and lunch tray. I really did have to get going—chem was starting in less than a minute. But now I was obliged to at least go over and say good-bye to the girl before I took off.

"My name's Alec," I said to her as I approached. "Alec Baines." I stood with my tray in one hand and my books pressed against my hip with the other.

"Nice to meet you, Alec. I'm Callie Mitchell." She held out her hand.

I set my tray down next to hers and shook her hand. "Nice to meet you," I said hastily. The bell was going to ring at any second, and I'd be late for my first chem class. "Sorry, but I really—"

Brrrng.

"Here, sit down in this chair, before some freshman comes along and tries to steal it," Callie said, patting the chair next to hers and tugging at my hand. "You're not a freshman, are you?"

"No." I sat down reluctantly. "I'm a senior."

"Me too, but I'm new around here. You must be an expert on Ellswood High by now." She took a small bite of hamburger and chewed it quickly. "Tell me all about it. I'm dying to get the dirt."

"There's not much to tell," I said. "It's like

14

any other high school, I guess. You have your jocks, your preps, your brains. . . ."

"Which are you, Alec?"

"Uh, well, none really, I guess."

"None *really*? You have to be something."

"I'm a regular senior, I guess." I couldn't tell this girl I'd just met that I was the biggest brain in the school. It would have seemed so obnoxious. And she *was* kind of cute.

"Uh-huh. Sure. Funny how everyone knows which clique everybody else belongs to, but no one ever admits to being part of one herself." She took a bite of hamburger. "Or himself."

"Hmm, yeah. Funny. I've noticed that."

She shot me a sidelong glance. "So how many courses did you get straight A's in last year?"

"Well, uh—all of them, actually." She was beginning to make me uncomfortable, even if she was cute. "I got a B freshman year, though. In wood shop. My birdhouse was crooked."

"I knew it!" she said with a laugh. "I could tell by looking at you. You're a total brain—only you're embarrassed to admit it."

"I'm not embarrassed. I didn't want to sound like I was bragging, that's all. Okay, so I'm a brain. What are you?"

"Who, me? I'm like everyone else." She took another small bite of hamburger. "I don't admit to being part of a clique."

"Journalism," I guessed. "You're on the school newspaper and your hero is Peter Jennings. I can 'tell by looking at you.'"

"Very good." She smiled. "But wrong. I couldn't care less about current events."

"Band?"

"Wrong again, bucko."

Theater? I hoped not. I hated actors. "Not cheerleading, I hope." I hated cheerleaders, too.

"What's wrong with cheerleading?" she asked. "But no, wrong again. Three strikes and you're out. And you've got to get going—you're already late for your chem class." The same mysterious smile returned, and something began to dawn on me.

I had been so busy trying to figure out those smiles that I hadn't noticed how pretty she really was. Not in the obvious, beach-bunny way of Lori Fordham, but in a different, almost exotic way. Her thick, dark-brown hair fell in loose, messy corkscrews onto her shoulders. She had a broad forehead and a wide mouth, and when she laughed, it seemed like you could see her teeth all the way back to her molars. Thick,

16

dark-brown eyebrows and eyelashes set off deep-green eyes, which were the slightest bit almond shaped. Her skin was a fine light tan, and she had one small mole on her right cheekbone. I realized with a start that this Callie person was the most beautiful girl I'd ever seen.

"How did you know I'm late for chem?" I asked her.

"First off, the loud groan you made when the bell rang was a pretty obvious hint that you were supposed to be somewhere else. Second, seeing as how your tray was empty when you sat down, either you're a mighty quick eater or you already sat through the first lunch shift. And third, you've been clutching that chem book like you're afraid it's going to fly away."

There was a silence of several seconds while I stared at her.

"Alec," she said. "Yoo-hoo. Remember chemistry? All those little beakers and burners? They're waiting for you. We don't want to put our GPA in jeopardy, now, do we?"

"Oh." I came back to reality. "Yeah. Right. I have to get going." I glanced down at my watch, then returned to staring at Callie. Suddenly, getting to chemistry on time no longer seemed so important. I wanted to keep talking to her, even if she was making fun of me. I didn't know what to say, though. I searched for something interesting or clever to keep the conversation going. "Will you be here tomorrow?" I blurted.

"I suppose so, unless I get expelled this afternoon." She smiled. "Will you skip chemistry again tomorrow to have lunch with me?"

"Sure! I mean, no—no, I can't do that. Look, Callie, why don't I meet you after school? I could show you around the place."

"Hmmm." She pretended to think it over. "You say you're an expert, eh? All right, it's a deal." She held out her hand once again. Before grasping it, I wiped a sweaty palm on my pant leg.

"Meet you at the front doors at three?" I asked.

"That would be great, Alec," she said. "At three. See you then."

"Yeah, see you." I gathered up my stuff and nodded good-bye.

Jogging through the empty halls to my chem class, for which I was now ten minutes late, I started laughing out loud.

Two

◆

So I met Callie in front at three. The early-September air had begun to get a little chilly, and she was now wearing a brown wool sweater over the turtleneck she'd had on earlier. Her thick hair was tied back in a ponytail. She smelled lightly of apples.

I was wearing my regular school uniform—high-tops, jeans, plain T-shirt and windbreaker, and my favorite blue Huskies cap with the big W, for Washington.

I took Callie on a tour of the school, pointing out to her places of historical interest, like the hall down which kids supposedly used to go streaking back in the seventies, and the corner

19

where Principal Gurties slipped and broke his wrist last year. He'd been chasing a dog that had wandered in. The jerk should have followed his own often-repeated advice about running in the halls.

As we walked around, Callie told me about herself. Her family had moved to Ellswood the week before. She'd liked their small town in Ohio, but hadn't minded too much when her father's company had transferred him to Washington. She thought of it as a new adventure. Callie was going out for the swim team. She played the harp.

"The harp?" I asked, perhaps with a bit of a snort.

"Sure. What's wrong with that?"

"Nothing. Nothing's *wrong* with it. It's just that I've never met anyone before who actually played the harp." I tried to make a joke of it. "I thought the only people who played the harp were Miss America candidates."

"Well, I play the harp, but I'm not planning a trip to Atlantic City anytime soon."

"Too bad. You'd look great in high heels and a bathing suit," I said teasingly.

"So would you," she shot back. "Especially in one of those little thongs."

We walked out to the football field. "This is where we'll be graduating next spring," I told her. "They set up a stage over there"—I pointed to the end zone at the far end of the field—"and all the seniors sit here."

"At my old high school, they held graduation in the gym."

"It's kind of nice to have it outside," I commented. "The valedictorian gives a little speech, the principal hands out the diplomas, and then everyone throws their caps in the air."

"I'm going to make funny faces at you while you're giving the valedictorian address," Callie said, wrinkling her nose at the imaginary stage in the end zone. "I'll make you laugh right in the middle of your speech."

"I'm not valedictorian yet," I reminded her.

"Oh, yeah, right. That *B* in freshman shop is going to drag you down."

"You never know. Anyway, if you make faces, I'll ignore you. I, for one, will maintain my dignity."

"Ignore me! Maintain your dignity!" Callie said. "Ha! You couldn't do either at lunch today, and you're not going to start now." She grabbed the Huskies cap off my head and started running across the field with it.

"Hey!" I took off after her.

I caught her under the goalposts and dragged her down onto the soft grass of the end zone, trying to wrestle the cap out of her hands.

"See, you can't ignore me," she said, giggling as I tickled her in the ribs. She let go of the cap, and I stuck it back on my head. "And I won't let you maintain your dignity around me, either." She tugged the bill down low so that it touched the tip of my nose.

My arms were half around Callie as we lay catching our breath from the wrestling match, and I could feel the bits of leaves and grass caught on her rough wool sweater, and her shoulder blades underneath. The woody odor of freshly cut grass mingled with the apple scent I had detected earlier. I must have looked pretty ridiculous, with my cap still pulled down all the way over my eyes, but I sensed that Callie was gazing at me. Though I couldn't see her face, I leaned toward her. Our lips met, and the Huskies cap, now caught between us, slowly lifted off my head and fell sideways to the ground. We ignored it for a long moment.

"Now, Callie, you have to tell me," I said finally. "If I'm a brain, what are you?"

Her reply was immediate. "A heart." And she

kissed me again, and though I wasn't sure exactly what she'd meant, somehow I knew she was right.

Soon we got up, brushed the twigs and leaves off our clothes and hair, and started hand-in-hand back toward the school. And just in time, too, because the football team was jogging out onto the field to practice.

Suddenly Callie stopped and let go of my hand. She was staring right through me, as if I wasn't there. An odd, fearful expression spread over her face.

"What's up?" I asked. Some of the football players were looking our way and snickering. It must have been pretty obvious what we'd been doing. "Don't pay any attention to those guys."

"What guys?" she said, still looking past me.

"Football players. Don't let the jerks bother you."

A couple of them were hooting and barking, and then Ruben Shiftman, the quarterback and star of the team, yelled, "Way to go, Baines!" What a comedian.

"Oh, them," Callie said, now meeting my eye. "Who cares what they think?" Still, she seemed upset over something.

"What's the matter?" I asked. "Are you feeling all right?"

"I'm fine, Alec," she said. "Really. I had the strangest feeling, that's all. I was thinking about how much fun it's going to be to graduate here next spring and how happy we'll be to get our diplomas. Then I got the worst feeling that it wasn't going to work out that way for either of us. You aren't going to give your valedictorian speech, and I'm not going to make funny faces at you. It's not going to happen at all."

"Well, it's certainly not going to happen if I keep showing up late to chemistry," I joked.

"No. I mean, it's really not going to happen." Callie turned to me, and her thick brown hair, which had begun to pull out of the ponytail, looked wild and disheveled. "Neither one of us is going to graduate."

I took her hand. "Don't be silly. Why would we flunk out?"

"Oh, Alec, that's not . . ." she started to reply, then trailed off. "Alec," she repeated, and clasped me hard around the chest.

"It's okay, Callie," I murmured into her hair as I held her. "It's okay."

Then the rhythm of the football players counting their jumping jacks began to fill the cool fall air. Silently Callie and I walked toward the school, the chant swelling behind us.

Three

I'd been working over the summer as an intern at CytoTek Incorporated in "downtown" Ellswood. The internship didn't pay that great—only minimum wage.

I could've made a lot more by being a lifeguard down at the lake or working on a logging crew, like a lot of the guys around Ellswood did over the summers. Those things would've been more fun, too—getting to be outside in the sun every day instead of holed up in an office.

But CytoTek was a pretty impressive name to have on my college applications. And since I was planning on med school, I couldn't pass it up. Now that school had started, I was working there part-time.

"Are you going in to CytoTek this morning?" my mother asked. It was a Saturday, a week and a half after the first day of school. Mom was sitting at the kitchen table, drinking a cup of coffee and reading the newspaper.

"Yeah. I haven't been going in that often, so I figured I'd go in today." I'd been spending most of my afternoons with Callie.

"Why don't you have some breakfast before you leave?" Mom asked.

"Good idea." I dug out a piece of coffee cake from the box on the counter with my hands.

"Use a fork," Mom said without looking up from her newspaper.

"Mmm-hmm." I opened the refrigerator and washed down the cake with some orange juice.

"And don't drink out of the carton."

"Right. Sorry." I put back the carton of juice and closed the refrigerator.

My mom had helped me get the internship in the first place. She's a graphic designer, and she'd been hired to create a new corporate logo for Cyto-Tek. When she got talking to the people there, she found out that they were looking for a reliable intern, and . . . next thing I knew, I was hired.

26

"Callie seems like a nice girl," my mother said out of the blue. They'd met a couple of days earlier, when Callie had come over after school. Being a freelance designer, Mom worked at home a lot for her clients in Seattle.

"Uh-huh. She's nice enough."

"Are you two dating?" She didn't look up from her newspaper.

"Sort of." It was embarrassing, talking to my mom about Callie. "We hang out together."

"That's nice. How are you doing with money?" Mom asked.

"Okay. Gas eats up a lot of it."

"Well, if you need any more—you know, to take Callie to a nice restaurant or something—you can ask me."

Mom sometimes helped me out when I was short of cash. "I'm fine, Mom. Really."

"I don't want you working too hard. All those awful rats at CytoTek!"

"The rats aren't too bad. You get used to them."

"I suppose." Mom looked at me. "I want you to have fun, that's all. It's your senior year."

"You sound like Ian." I did an imitation of Ian on cruise control.

"Well, Ian knows what he's talking about. And so do I. Next year you go off to college, and you'll have to get serious. But for now—no worries, no problems. This should be the happiest time of your life."

Mom had kind of an unrealistic view of high school. "I'll be fine. I'm having fun." I picked up three oranges and tried to juggle them. After a couple of tosses, they clunked on the floor. "Fun, see?"

"I see a young man who'd better enjoy life while he can," Mom said seriously, bending over in her chair to pick up the oranges.

I snatched one out of her hands and tossed it in the air to myself. "Gotta go." I headed out of the kitchen, then turned and said, "Oh, and Mom? Message received."

She smiled. "Good."

CytoTek was a small company specializing in biotechnology—genetic engineering, mainly. It was down on Main Street—yes, Ellswood's main street is named Main Street—on the seventh floor of the ComFax Tower, otherwise known as the RoboCop Building.

Everyone called it the RoboCop Building because it looked like the skyscrapers in the movie *RoboCop*—all sharp angles, matte-gray steel, and black glass. It wasn't much of a skyscraper, actually. Only in Ellswood, Washington, would a nine-story building be called a tower. But it really stuck out among all the old two- and three-story red-brick and sandstone buildings along Main Street. And it was the only one I could remember *not* being there.

The other intern at CytoTek, Hillis Milner, and I had the very glamorous chore of feeding the lab rats and cleaning out their cages. We had to make sure that all the bottles were filled with fresh water every other day and that the little critters never ran out of rodent chow.

The paper underneath their cages had to be changed twice weekly—this for over six hundred rats in almost as many cages. It was too much work for me and Hillis alone, so there was a rotating schedule that included some of the regular building janitors—who were paid time and a half to do it, by the way. It certainly wasn't the greatest job ever—in fact, it was pretty gross—but I too got fringe benefits.

In exchange for my good work with the rats, I was given unlimited access to CytoTek's computers. My mom had a graphics computer at home, on which she did most of her designing, and I'd become pretty comfortable with it. But CytoTek had heavy-duty computers that made my mom's machine seem like an abacus. CytoTek's system had more power than most hackers even dream about.

I got my other big perk by becoming a bit of a pet to the doctors. Everyone at CytoTek had at least one Ph.D., so they were all called doctors, though I wouldn't have trusted any of them to set a splint. It's an old joke, the absentminded professor, but it was true at CytoTek. Those people were geniuses, every one of them, but outside their area of expertise, they were complete incompetents.

Dr. Pensall, for instance, was practically helpless. She had a Ph.D. in chemistry from Cal Tech and one in biology from Johns Hopkins, and I had to show her how to put the filters in her new coffeemaker.

The docs liked me because I could do that sort of thing for them. I was the one who figured out the problem when Dr. Larsten couldn't get his radiation spectrometer to work. He and two other doctors had been puzzling over it for an hour. They didn't bat an eye when I pointed out that the machine was unplugged.

After a couple of weeks, enough of the doctors owed me little favors that when I hinted around about doing something more substantial than wiping up rat dung, they let me have my own lab.

It wasn't exactly a real laboratory—actually, it was a converted broom closet. But after I spent a week hanging shelves and putting in new overhead lights, it was more than serviceable. There wasn't much space, but it had room for cages and a desk and computer terminal for me to work at.

Late in the summer, CytoTek bought a bunch of new rats, and I was given thirty-five of them to use in my own experiment.

That Saturday, however, I took my mom's advice and didn't work too hard. I quickly took care of the rats under my name on the rotating schedule, plus checked in on my own rats. Everyone was fine.

I was going swimming in the afternoon. Ian and Gina hadn't met Callie before, and I was a little nervous about how everyone would get along.

I made the introductions as we stood in the gravel lot outside the lake. "Callie Mitchell, this is Ian Golder and Gina Phelps. Gina, Ian—Callie."

"I'm so happy to meet you," Gina said. "Alec's told us so much about you."

"Is that so?" Callie said pleasantly. "All good, I hope."

"Of course." Gina took me by the arm and started walking me to the lake. Ian and Callie followed us.

"Well," Gina whispered to me.

"'Well' what?"

"'Well' nothing. She certainly is pretty."

"Yeah, she is. And nice too. And smart. And—"

"Okay, Alec, I get the picture."

We walked in silence for a few seconds. I could hear Callie and Ian chatting behind us. They seemed to be hitting it off great.

"She's very tall," Gina said thoughtfully.

"Uh-huh. About five eight, I guess." Gina was only five three or so.

"And I love her hair. I always wished mine curled naturally into ringlets like that."

"Gina, you have nice hair."

"Nice? Nice! It's not curly, though. It's—"

"You're jealous, aren't you?" I asked, laughing. By now Callie and Ian had fallen far enough behind us that we could talk loudly without being overheard.

"Of course not. Why would I—"

"Ha! For all your talk of finding me a girlfriend, here you are—"

"I am not jealous." She slapped my arm.

"No, no," I teased. "Certainly not."

"I'm happy for you."

"I'm sure you are."

"And Callie seems very sweet."

"I'm sure she does."

"But when I said you should get a girlfriend, I didn't mean get one like *her*! She's gorgeous. Of course I'm jealous. I look like a sack of potatoes next to her."

"Don't be silly, Gina." I slung my arm over her shoulder. "Callie or no Callie, you know I'll always have a secret crush on you."

"You mean that?"

"You know I do." I squeezed her shoulder a little.

"Thanks. I'll always have a crush on you, too."

Ian and Callie walked up a few seconds later. They were kidding each other and laughing like old friends. We put out our towels and stripped down to our bathing suits. Ian and Gina decided to go for a swim right away, while Callie and I stretched out on our backs.

"Ian and Gina seem nice," Callie said.

"Yeah, they're good guys."

"Ian mentioned you've known each other since grade school," she said thoughtfully. "You're lucky to have such an old friend."

"I guess so. I'd never really thought about it."

"I don't have anyone who goes back that far."

"No?"

"Not anymore."

"What do you mean, not anymore?" I asked.

"Oh, you know." She shrugged. "Friends move, or change. You lose people along the way."

"But you can always keep in touch," I said. "I still write letters to a guy who moved away in fifth grade."

"You can't *always* write letters, Alec," she said stiffly. Almost harshly.

What was the matter with her?

I was about to ask her, when she rolled onto her stomach. She turned her face away from me.

End of conversation.

By the next weekend, it seemed as if Callie and I had been together forever. We'd spent every afternoon after school together, and all day Saturday and Sunday. When we weren't together, it was all I could do not to think about her, and when we were together, half the time we didn't say anything—we just sort of sat there basking in each other's company.

Some days we would go over to her house

after school and she'd practice the harp for me. I'd lie down on the couch in the living room and close my eyes and listen to her make music—incredible music, like I'd never heard before.

Listening to her do her scales, humming them lightly, so low that I wasn't sure it was her I was hearing or the strings' own harmonic echo, was enough to put me in a trance. Sometimes I'd actually slip into a dream.

I never believed that the devil carries a pitchfork, but listening to Callie play made me see why the harp was the angels' musical instrument of choice.

On other days we'd hike the Burlington Trail, a small state park that bordered Ellswood. A twelve-mile "nature trail" winding through a thick forest of old-growth hemlocks and firs, it was popular with joggers. I sometimes ran it myself.

It rains almost every day in this part of Washington, but it rarely rains hard. Usually a constant misting. We'd wander hand-in-hand off the trail, through stands of ancient trees, trying to catch on our tongues the occasional fat droplet that plunged down from the canopy above, until we were so dizzy from looking straight up that we fell over in a pile of laughter.

Callie would bring her camera—an old Kodak Brownie—and take pictures of me. I'd shoot her, too, trying to capture the way the mist frizzed up her hair and formed glistening droplets in it like dew in a spider's web.

But my photos never came out. I could never get the hang of the Brownie's manual settings—I was used to my mom's all-automatic Nikon for the photographically impaired. My pictures of Callie were almost always overexposed or out of focus, or else her head or feet were cut off.

Callie's photos of me, though, were small works of art, despite their unworthy subject. In picture after picture, there I'd be, my ugly mug in unfortunately precise focus, framed by intensely green ferns or dark-red tree bark so alive looking as to make me seem waxen in comparison.

So Callie would take these incredible photographs—of me, of the woods, of rocks and streams, of everything—and insist on giving them to me.

"Callie, I can't accept these," I said to her, fanning out the photos in my hands. "They're yours. You took them. You should keep them."

"That's okay, Alec. I want you to have them. Consider them a present."

"Why don't you want them? If I'd taken them, I know I wouldn't give them away."

"I just don't want them," she said lightly. Then, folding up the fan of pictures in my hands and pushing them toward me, she added, "Here. They're yours."

"Callie, I really can't—"

"Enough," she said, and pressed her forefinger to my lips. "Please keep them."

And so I would. Soon I had quite a collection stashed away in the sock drawer of my dresser.

Callie had been taking up almost all of my time. I'd been neglecting my work at CytoTek—both my regular chores with the rats and my own experiment. But I couldn't bear to leave Callie even for a single afternoon, so I'd asked Hillis Milner, the other intern, to take up my slack. Finally, though, I had to go in to check up on things, and I had the brilliant idea of asking Callie to come along.

It was a warm day, and I had the top down on the car. My green Triumph was more than twenty years old—nearly enough to qualify for antique-auto plates. I'd bought it over a year ago from a student at Anselm State, the local college. The car was in decent shape overall, but still the thing was constantly breaking down. The student didn't have the time or know-how to fix it himself, and he couldn't afford to take it to a garage. So he sold it to me cheap to get rid of it.

I liked tinkering with it. On the one hand, because it was so old, there was always something going wrong with it. On the other, it had been built in the days before computers were put into cars, and it was a surprisingly simple little machine. There wasn't a whole lot that could go wrong that I couldn't fix myself. It hardly ever saw the inside of T.J.'s repair shop. And I knew exactly what it could and couldn't do on the road.

When I roared up to her house, Callie was waiting on the front stoop. She was wearing khaki shorts and a navy-blue sweatshirt. Her hair was tied back in a tight braid so it wouldn't get too blown around when we drove. She looked great, as always.

We blasted the radio all the way to the RoboCop Building's parking lot.

"Whew!" Callie said as we stepped off the elevator on the seventh floor of the RoboCop Building. "I can smell the rats from here."

"You get used to it after a while," I said. "I don't even notice it anymore."

Running my I.D. card through an electronic sensor, I pointed to a large blue-and-white sign saying CYTOTEK INCORPORATED on the glass door. "That's the logo my mom designed," I said.

"Neat," said Callie. "Your mom must be really creative."

"Yeah, she is," I said, pushing through the heavy door quickly before it stopped beeping. "Come on. Let me show you around."

From the outside, the RoboCop Building looked ultramodern, but once you got past the lobby, it looked pretty shabby. At least CytoTek's floor did.

There was a large, open room with various pieces of machinery—microscopes, centrifuges, oscilloscopes—scattered around on tables and in cases. Off the main laboratory were three corridors, down which were the private offices and smaller labs of the various researchers.

"Looks kind of junky," said Callie. "I expected it to be more . . . sleek, or something."

"Yeah," I said, picking a Butterfinger wrapper and an empty Snapple bottle off of a beta analyzer and tossing them in the garbage can in the corner. "There's hundreds of thousands of dollars' worth of equipment lying around here, but you'd never know it."

"Show me your lab," she said.

"It's not really a lab, you know."

"Don't be modest, Alec. Let me see the place where the future Nobel Prize winner is going to find the cure for cancer."

"It's down this—"

"Nobel Prize!" came a voice from a nearby office. "In your dreams." Hillis Milner loped into the room. "Glad you finally showed, Baines. I'm getting tired of cleaning up after your stinky rats."

Like Callie and me, Hillis was a senior at Ellswood High. He was tall—over six three—and had greasy brown bangs and a long face. He walked with this funny bobbing motion, as if he was a short guy trapped in an elongated body he hadn't quite learned how to steer. I always had an urge to call him "dude," a word I never used.

"Callie, this is Hillis Milner. He's also an intern here," I said, ignoring his remarks. "Hillis, this is Callie Mitchell."

"Nice to meet you," said Callie, shaking his hand.

"Yeah, same here, babe," Hillis replied, looking her up and down. He squinted at her. "Mitchell, eh? I think my mom works with one of your relatives. Doreen Mitchell?"

"Yes, that's my aunt."

"Yeah. Your aunt. So I heard about why you moved here."

"My father was transferred," Callie said stiffly.

"Uh-huh." Hillis jerked his head to the left to throw the bangs out of his eyes, and bobbed up and down. "Say, Baines, are you gonna be coming in anymore? 'Cause if you're not, I could use your lab."

"Sorry, Hillis, not planning on quitting yet. But thanks for covering for me last week."

"No problem. You owe me."

"Right. Catch you later," I said, leading Callie down the corridor to my lab.

"See you. See you, too, Callie," Hillis said with a leer.

When we got out of earshot, Callie said, "Charming creep, that Hillis. You didn't tell me you had such a pleasant co-worker."

"You get used to him, too," I said, rolling my eyes. "I try to ignore him, mainly. What was all that about your aunt Doreen?"

"Oh, nothing. Just a gossipy relative of mine who works with his mom, like he said."

"Oh."

"What did Hillis mean when he said he could use your lab?"

"Well, you know how I was given a broom closet to fix up? Hillis laughed at first, but then when he saw that it didn't make a half-bad workspace, he asked for one too. Unfortunately, there weren't any more spare closets, so Hillis got set up in the main room back there—those were his rats in the corner. He's made it no secret that he thinks the doctors were playing favorites, and that he wouldn't mind having my closet now that I've fixed it up."

We'd arrived at the door to my lab. "And here we are," I said, opening the door and flicking on the lights.

"Alec, this is really nice," Callie said, stepping into the tiny room and looking around. "Especially for a broom closet. I'm impressed." She stuck a finger into one of the rat cages and made a clicking sound. "They won't bite, will they?"

"Those guys? Nah. They're gentle as kittens."

"What are you doing with them? I mean, what is your experiment about?"

"It's kind of complicated, but basically I'm trying to find a natural antifreeze."

"What do you mean, antifreeze?" she said,

42

picking up one of the rats and stroking his white fur.

"For organ transplants." I began changing the water bottles and refilling the food trays. "Say you needed a kidney, and the only kidney available was in Florida. If you're too sick to jump on a plane, you'd be out of luck. It's very difficult to transport organs. They go bad too quickly. And you can't freeze them for storage, because cold temperatures damage them. What I'm trying to do is find a chemical that will let you freeze an organ without damaging it in any way, so that there'll be more time for organs and the people who need them to get together."

"Huh. So where're you going to find this chemical? It sounds pretty impossible," Callie said as she let the rat climb up onto her shoulder.

"Again, it's sort of complicated. See, there are plenty of deep-sea fish that swim around in freezing-cold water that would turn you and me into ice cubes in ten seconds. And these fish aren't like whales or seals, which have thick blubber to keep them warm. These fish are cold all the way through, and they live just fine. Something in their bodies makes it possible—a natural antifreeze."

I'd finished changing the paper underneath all the cages, and I picked up one of the rats and cupped him in my hands. "I'm immersing rat organs with various fish proteins, trying to isolate that antifreeze."

"Wait a second," Callie said, plucking the rat from her shoulder. "How are you doing that?"

"Well, first I kill them, then—"

"Kill them! How can you *kill* them?" She held the rat against her chest protectively. "They're so cute!"

"Callie, I can't tell how their organs are holding up to cold temperatures if they're still alive. They have to be dead first, and *then* I can do my experiments."

"Oh, Alec, that's awful. Look at their innocent little pink eyes. How can you stand to execute them?"

"Sorry, but you wouldn't mind it so much if you were in desperate need of a new kidney and my experiment was going to save your life."

"I guess so. Anyway, I'm sure you don't enjoy having to kill them. What do you do, give them poison or something?"

"You don't want to know."

I couldn't tell her that poison in a rat's bloodstream would throw off the results of any experiment. Lab rats had to be killed quickly and cleanly, and the easiest way to do it was by grabbing them around the middle and smashing them headfirst onto a table. Kind of sickening the first few times you heard their necks snap, but you got used to it—and it was very effective.

"You're right, I don't want to know." Callie placed the rat back in his cage. "Sorry, little fellow," she said to the rat, "but your noble sacrifice may save my life someday."

There was an awkward silence for a moment.

I coughed. "Let's hope nothing like that ever happens." I started to put my rat away too.

"Well, if it ever does," Callie said, "don't let them try *too* hard to save me. I don't want to end up a vegetable." She grinned. "All things considered, I'd rather be dead. So remember to pull the plug on me."

"Can't we talk about something more pleasant?" I asked.

"Sure. So what's that Hillis guy working on for his experiment? He probably likes murdering his rats."

We walked out of the lab, and I flicked the light off and shut the door behind us. "I hate to say this, but for his experiment the rats have to be alive."

"Alec! So while you're doing in your poor defenseless rats, that creep Hillis is letting his live. Why don't you do an experiment like his?"

"Callie, my rats are better off dead than his are alive. He's doing some sort of work with growth hormones—he won't tell anyone what it is, exactly. But his rats have all become bloated giants. They look like furry white basketballs. It's pretty sad, actually."

"Yuck. Can't you come up with an experiment where the rats are alive *and* healthy?"

"No such luck. Anyway, I'm not sure what the point of Hillis's gigantic rats is"—I lowered my voice as we entered the main laboratory—"but I have some ideas."

Hillis was standing near the front door, whispering angrily at a guy in shorts and an Anselm State sweatshirt with an insignia of crossed oars. When Hillis saw us, he stopped talking and quickly stuffed something into the kid's hand. Then he started hustling him toward the door that led to the elevator.

"What's all this about?" Callie muttered under her breath.

"I'll tell you in a sec," I whispered back. Then, loudly, to Hillis: "Hey, dude, we're taking

46

off. Thanks again for covering for me." Callie and I headed for the door.

"Sure, right, Baines," he replied, now pulling the kid in the Anselm sweatshirt back into the room. Hillis evidently didn't want the three of us to ride in the elevator together. "Nice meeting you, babe," he said to Callie's back as we walked out.

"You too, *babe*," Callie said as the door swung shut behind us.

We stood silently waiting for the elevator as Hillis and the other kid eyed us nervously through the glass door.

Finally, in the privacy of the elevator, Callie exploded. "I'm gonna smack that goofball next time he calls me 'babe'! And why was he acting so paranoid?"

"Remember I told you he was experimenting with growth hormones on his rats? He's cagey about it, but I'm pretty sure he's manufacturing steroids for human use. There've been lots of jocks sniffing around CytoTek lately—body-builders, athletes from Anselm State, even some of the guys on Ellswood's football team. Hillis seems to have a booming business."

"Nice," Callie commented dryly. "Is that what he was doing when we walked in?"

"Maybe. I noticed the guy he was talking to was wearing an Anselm State Crew sweatshirt."

The elevator door opened, and we stepped into the slick marble lobby of the RoboCop Building. "In any case," I said, "I try to steer clear of Hillis and his sleazy business. But I do feel sorry for his rats."

Four

It had been about a month since school had started and I'd met Callie, and I still hadn't learned why she'd freaked out on the football field that first day. I'd tried to bring up the subject a couple of times, and she seemed unwilling to discuss it. It really bothered me—it was as if she was hiding something from me.

Besides running the Burlington Trail every now and then, I lifted weights three times a week after school. I was keeping in shape for the spring track season. I wasn't a great sprinter, and I didn't have terrific endurance, but I was pretty tall and had good flexibility.

Even knowing this about myself, as a freshman I had dreams of competing in the glory events—the 100-meter dash or the metric mile. Coach Leyritz took one look at my times, however, and made a 400-meter hurdler and backup relay man of me. Oh, well. At least I was on the team, and I lettered my junior year.

Callie was on the swim team. She had gone out for the hardest events in her sport too and had made them, natch. She swam the 100-meter freestyle and 200-meter medley and was the last leg of the 400-meter relay.

Ellswood High wasn't the fanciest school in the world, but it did have an indoor swimming pool with a whirlpool attached, and a sauna.

After lifting weights and changing into my swim trunks, I met Callie in the sauna.

"Ah, this feels great," I said, pouring some water over the hot rocks, then stretching out on one of the low wooden benches.

"I'm beat," said Callie. She spread her towel on a nearby bench and lay down on it. She was wearing her swim-team suit—an industrial-strength black one-piece.

"How many laps did you do today?"

"Almost a hundred, total."

"Geez. I sink like a stone after five."

"That's 'cause you thrash around so much,"

Callie said. "You probably use up more energy swimming five laps than I do in fifty. No offense, Alec, but you're a terrible swimmer."

"Thanks loads, Cal," I said. My voice became serious, and I turned the subject to what I'd been thinking about for weeks: "I want to know what happened that first day. On the football field."

Callie said nothing for a moment. Then, "Please, let's drop it. Okay?"

"You were acting really weird, Callie. Not like you."

"I can't talk about it, Alec."

"You can't? Or you won't?"

"Can't, won't, what's the difference?"

"It may not make any difference to you, but it does to me."

"Alec—" Her voice cracked. "Please don't ask me . . ."

"I just did."

She was silent for a good minute. The sauna's automatic heater turned itself on and off with loud clicks.

"Alec, ever since I was a little girl, I've gotten these feelings—like I know things."

"Know things? How do you mean?" Even though it must have been 110 degrees in the sauna, I went cold all over. I could feel the goose bumps rising on my arms.

"Oh, it doesn't make much sense."

"You think you're psychic?"

"I know it sounds ridiculous, like I bend spoons or something," Callie said. "But yes, sometimes I do know what's going to happen before it actually does."

"Like what?"

"Like bad things. I dream about people."

"I dream about people too. So?"

"I dream about people dying."

"Callie, that happens to everybody now and then."

"But my dreams come true."

I didn't want to tell her she was full of it, but I didn't believe this psychic-dream business for a second.

"You think I'm crazy, don't you?" Callie asked.

"Not crazy."

"Or imagining things."

"Well . . ."

"I don't imagine it. Sometimes I have dreams—"

"Callie, everyone has dreams like that. You know. You have a dream about a car wreck.

Then you read in the paper the next morning about someone who was killed in a traffic accident. It seems like your dream was psychic—but it wasn't, see? People are killed every day in car crashes. You might as well say you're psychic for knowing that the sun is going to rise."

"Alec, I can tell the difference between knowing the sun is going to rise and knowing—" She stopped.

"Knowing what?"

"Knowing your own sister is going to die," she finished. Before I could say anything, she went on. "I'm sorry I haven't told you about Jessie before, Alec. I just couldn't." There was another long pause. "My family didn't move to Ellswood because my father was transferred."

"Oh?" I remembered Hillis saying something about that.

"We moved here to be with my aunt Doreen. No, that's not really true. Daddy chose Ellswood because his sister lives here, but the real reason we moved was to get away. From Ohio. From the memories."

"I don't under—"

"I'm sorry, Alec. For not telling you before. It's hard for me to talk about."

I sat silently.

"Even though Jessie was four years older than I was," she began again, "we were very close. I followed her around everywhere. She never told me to bug off the way some big sisters do. We used to go out and take pictures together—Jessie loved photography. From the time I was old enough to walk, practically, she had me out tramping around taking pictures. That's why I know how to use a camera so well. Oh, and Alec—if you think my pictures are good, you should have seen Jessie's. She had this amazing . . ."

Callie's voice broke off.

"We used to rent videos together," she continued, "and then act out the scenes. Jessie loved those old black-and-white movies." She paused again. Though I couldn't see her through the steam, I knew she was smiling.

"Anyway, last spring Jessie was at college—she was a junior in the film school at U.C.L.A. People were always saying she was pretty enough to be a movie star, but she was too smart for that. . . . She wanted to be behind the camera—a cinematographer, maybe direct someday. Oh, Alec, you would've loved her—everyone did."

"Tell me what happened," I urged.

"Jessie was making a short movie about a woman named Peg Entwhistle. Peg Entwhistle

54

was a frustrated actress back in the thirties who committed suicide by jumping off the *H* in the famous 'Hollywood' sign. Jessie loved that sort of story. Her idea was to make a kind of fake documentary of Peg Entwhistle's life, called *Death of a Starlet*. She herself would play Peg.

"Then I started having the dreams. Every night for weeks and weeks, I dreamed Jessie was standing beneath a giant, lit-up movie marquee that spelled out 'Hollywood' in the same crooked pattern as the famous sign. She was wearing a slinky white gown and one of those old-fashioned hats that look like bathing caps. I'll never forget how she looked in the dream—so glamorous, so happy. And I was happy for her.

"Then the dream turned into a nightmare. The marquee exploded. Flames everywhere, smoke, broken glass showering down on her. She tried to run, but it was as if she was paralyzed, rooted to the spot. It all seemed to be taking place in slow motion, and I couldn't move to help her either, and I saw Jessie bleeding and—"

I sat up, searching for Callie. She was only a vague outline in the mist.

Callie continued. "Jessie had told me she was going to be filming in L.A. up at the 'Hollywood' sign. I thought my dream meant that she would be in danger there. I told her to be careful. Of course she laughed it off, and when she was finished shooting and nothing had happened, I felt pretty stupid. But I still couldn't help thinking that the dream was trying to tell me something.

"At the end of the semester Jessie screened the film for her classmates and instructors. She got permission to show it at a huge, condemned movie palace in downtown L.A. It was the perfect place for the opening of a film about a down-and-out thirties starlet. The theater was packed. As a lark, Jessie dressed for the screening in the long white gown she'd worn as Peg Entwhistle."

The air was stifling in the sauna. We'd stayed in too long, and I was beginning to feel light-headed. Callie's words faded in and out.

"There was a fire in the theater that night— started by the ancient wiring, they said later. The place lit up like a match. The lights went down—smoke, confusion, screams, people running over each other to get out. In that tight gown, Jessie never had a chance."

The heater ticked on and off.

"They identified her body by the dental records," she said flatly. "Oh, and at the last moment, Jessie had retitled her film. She called it *Hollywood*."

I went over and sat down heavily next to Callie. I was woozy from the short walk. "I'm sorry." I knew it sounded lame, but what else could I say?

"The dream had been telling me Jessie would die in a fire at a theater where her movie was showing," Callie said. "But it was more than the dream. For weeks before the accident, I knew—I just knew—that Jessie was in danger. I had known all along that she was going to die, and how, and I couldn't stop it from happening."

Okay. The story was pretty weird. I could see how it might have seemed to Callie like she had ESP or something. But there had to be another explanation. Coincidence, or whatever.

"Alec, don't you see?" Callie asked. "We're in danger. I know it. I could feel it, that day on the football field. And we won't be able to stop it, no matter what we do. You can't avoid fate. I know it. I know it with all my soul."

I was tired. I wanted to get out of that sauna. "Callie, listen to yourself. Nothing bad is going to happen to us. I'm sorry Jessie died." I reached out and took her hand in mine. Her flesh was burning. "You have to look at it rationally. We're perfectly safe."

"Maybe you're right, Alec," she said, unconvinced. "Maybe I'm still shook up over Jessie."

"I can understand that." I stroked her hair, which was in tighter corkscrews than usual because of the steam. "It must have been terrible for you and your family."

"It was," she said simply. "Dad has never really been the same."

She got up to go, and I gratefully slung my towel over my shoulder and started after her.

We were heading down the corridor toward the locker rooms when someone called out, "Hey, Baines, wait up."

Hillis Milner stood in the doorway to the weight room, shifting his tall, lanky body nervously from foot to foot. I could see Ruben Shiftman and four or five other football players multiplied in the mirrors lining the weight room. Evidently Hillis wasn't at the gym to work out—he was still in his street clothes.

"Hey, what's up?" I asked.

"Nothing much, man. What's up with you?"

"Nothing much." *Dude*, I added silently.

There was a silence of several seconds, and then he turned to Callie. "What's up with you, babe?" Hillis wasn't exactly a great conversationalist.

58

"Nothing much, *babe*," she said. "What's up with you?"

"Nothing much," Hillis repeated, continuing to rock back and forth. "Nothing much at all."

"Well, Hillis, it's been nice talking with you." I began moving on.

"Yo, wait up, man," he said.

I looked at him expectantly.

"You're gonna be going out for the track team in a couple of months."

"Yeah, that's right, Hillis. I'll probably be running hurdles, same as last year."

"You'd rather run sprints."

"I guess so. Not really." What was it to him?

"You need to start training now if you want to beat O'Connor in the hundred meter."

"Hurdles are okay. Besides, I'm keeping in shape."

"You could be in better shape."

"Thanks a lot, Hillis. Look, I gotta go change." I started to walk away. "I'll see you la—"

Suddenly Hillis lurched forward and clutched my arm. "Wait up, Baines," he said, tossing his hair back with a jerk of his head. "Wait up," he repeated.

I was getting tired of his bull. "Hillis, what is your problem?"

"No problem with me, man. You have the problem. I have the solution."

It was beginning to dawn on me what this was all about. Hillis wanted to sell me some of the stuff he made in his laboratory.

"No, thanks, Hillis." I started to walk away again, but Hillis gripped my arm tighter and pulled his long face down close to mine. His breath smelled like cheddar cheese.

"Man, you haven't even heard the solution yet," he muttered. "I can provide you with some performance boosters that'll have O'Connor eating your dust."

"'Performance boosters,'" I said dryly. "You mean steroids. No, thanks."

"Hey, man, keep it down. I'm doing you a personal favor."

"That's real nice of you, Hillis, but I pass."

"Are you sure, man? Maybe your girlfriend would be interested," he said, still grasping my arm.

"You'll have to ask her, dude," I said. "And I'm giving you five seconds to let go of my arm before I throw you through that wall." I smiled pleasantly at him.

Ignoring me, he turned to Callie. "Hey, you're on the swim team." He leered at her, bobbing his head up and down. "You're in fine shape, but I could shape you up even more."

"Buzz off, creep," Callie said.

"Look, b—*oomph!*"

Hillis's five seconds had expired, and he still hadn't released my arm. Slamming his chest with the palm of my free hand, I grabbed a handful of T-shirt and drove him against the wall.

I really hadn't shoved him very hard. After all, I still had to work with the guy at CytoTek. And now that he'd finally let go of my arm, I let go of his shirt and stepped back.

That was when Hillis went ballistic. His pimply face turned pink as a rat's eye. He was literally shaking with rage. He clenched and unclenched his fists and bobbed up and down.

"You're dead!" he screeched at me. "You're dead!" Then he started cursing Callie and me so violently that spit was foaming down his chin.

I was completely shocked, and I had to stop myself from laughing. I was sure I hadn't hurt him. I'd even given him fair warning that I was going to *make* him let go of me. And I noticed that despite his threats, he hadn't tried to hit me back.

"Geez, Hillis, take it easy—" I began.

Then Hillis surprised me by lunging at me, windmilling his long arms wildly. I ducked and grappled him around the chest, lifting him off the floor. Now what was I going to do with him?

The next thing I knew, Ruben Shiftman and a couple of his buddies were prying us apart, with Hillis kicking his size thirteens at me as they dragged him away.

"What's all of this about, Baines?" Ruben asked me, poking me in the chest with his forefinger. He was taking on the righteous tone that bullies assume when moved to defend the weak.

"They hit me!" Hillis screamed, pointing at me and Callie.

That was so ridiculous that I couldn't help but burst out laughing. Callie stifled a giggle.

"What's so funny, Baines?" Ruben poked at me again.

"Ruben, lay off before I snap your finger in half," I said.

"Oh yeah? Oh yeah?" Ruben said, but he didn't poke me. Although he was captain of the football team, he wasn't that big. I had a good two inches and ten pounds on him. "You lay off of Hillis, you hear? He's a friend of mine."

All of a sudden Hillis, Ruben, and the other football players parted silently and began slinking back toward the weight room. I turned and saw Mr. Beerman, who taught psychology and sociology, as well as "health," coming up the hall.

"Problem, gentlemen?" He hiked up his pants, which were drooping low on his hips. He looked at Callie. "Lady?"

"No, no problem," Callie replied coolly.

"I thought I heard a little disturbance," Mr. Beerman said. "You know how Mr. Gurties dislikes disturbances. You know how Mr. Gurties likes to run a *tight ship*."

"No problem," Hillis muttered at the door to the weight room. "No disturbance."

"Good," Mr. Beerman said, clapping his hands together and rubbing them. "Good. See that there isn't," he added, turning on his heel and going back the direction he'd come.

"What a loser," I said to Callie.

"Really," she agreed.

Hillis, Ruben, and the rest of the guys shuffled into the weight room without another word.

"C'mon." I steered Callie down the hall. When we were at the door to the boys' locker room, far enough away that Hillis wouldn't be able to hear me, I burst out laughing. "I can't believe Hillis actually took a swing at me—I didn't think he had it in him."

"He didn't," Callie said. "Ruben and the other guys were already at the door of the weight room when he tried to hit you. He knew they'd be there to separate you."

"Figures. And seeing as how Ruben stuck up for him, you gotta figure something's in it for him."

Callie squinted. "You think Ruben's using Hillis's 'performance boosters'?"

"What do you think?" I asked. Then, before pushing through the locker-room door, I added, "And judging from the way Hillis lost it back there, I'd say he's been sampling the product himself."

Five

◆

The next day I saw Hillis loping around the halls in school. He shot me some dirty looks from beneath his greasy brown bangs, but he didn't say anything. He was too busy pushing his "performance boosters" to all the jocks at Ellswood.

When Ruben Shiftman and his buddies were pulling us apart, Hillis had screamed over and over that he was going to "get" me. It seemed like a pretty vague threat. But since Hillis probably was using his homemade steroids, there was no telling how many pistons he was firing on. And he'd never been the most stable guy, mentally speaking. Callie was worried that he was actually going to try something.

I'd known Hillis for years, and I had a pretty good idea of what the guy was capable of: not much. He'd lost it that day, but really—what could he do to me?

It was already dark when I pulled up to the RoboCop Building that Thursday evening. The floodlit bushes around its base glowed with a silvery sheen as I turned off the Triumph's ignition and coasted into my usual parking space. The lot was empty.

Normally I wouldn't have been going to CytoTek at night, but that afternoon there'd been a preseason meeting of the track team that had held me over. I didn't want to get behind on my lab work. I had made some real progress in the tissue-preservation experiment.

I slid my I.D. through the electronic pass guard next to the lobby entrance. Hearing the *click* of the lock unlatching, I quickly pushed through the glass door.

As I walked through the deserted lobby, the echo of my footsteps disturbed the perfect marble silence. I had an uncanny sense that I was intruding on its privacy. My presence introduced a sloppy, unpredictable, *human* element to its smooth surfaces and calculated angles. What if I spray-painted my name on the reception desk? Threw an egg on the ceiling? Turned a cartwheel?

The elevator door closed behind me with a sigh of relief, and the Robocop Building, glad to rid its pristine lobby of the intruder, whisked me to the seventh floor.

All the lights except the dim wall sconces were off at CytoTek. I paused in the large front room, allowing my eyes to adjust to the low light.

Most rodents are more active at night than during the day, and I could hear the high squeaks of dozens of caged rats. The faint *tap-tap* as they dabbed at their water bottles. The scratching of tiny paws on wire mesh.

I picked my way carefully down the darkened hallways to my broom-closet laboratory.

The door to the lab was unlatched—funny, I was always careful to pull it shut behind me. Must have been the cleaning lady.

There was a brief burst of scurrying and squeaking in the cages lining the wall when the lights flicked on. "Hey, guys," I said aloud to the rats. "Miss me?" They didn't respond. "Nope, I guess not."

I moved over to my desk and turned on the computer, which immediately bathed the small room in an amber glow. The file that kept track of which rats were due next to be experimented on came up. Rats Eleven, Twelve, and Thirteen.

When I first started at the lab, I named the rats I was working with. Ratman, Ratcliffe, Rathbone, and so on. But soon I discovered that it was much more difficult to kill them if they had names. They began to seem like pets or something. It was better to keep it impersonal. Also, I was running out of clever names.

Numbers Eleven through Thirteen were on the highest of the five shelves along the wall, and I had to scoot my desk chair over and climb up onto it to reach their cage.

"Sorry, boys," I said as I lifted their cage off the shelf.

That was when all hell broke loose.

The shelf gave way beneath the cage I was holding and the light fixture overhead flashed and banged and came swinging down. In the sudden disorienting dark I felt the shelves on the wall collapsing into me, knocking me off the swivel chair. I tried to brace myself for impact with the concrete floor.

Wham! I hit the floor with a heavy smack.

Somehow I managed to land mainly on my shoulder and side without knocking myself unconscious. Wrapping my arms around my head, I squeezed my eyes shut and hoped that none of the heavy shelves cracked my head open. Light fixtures continued to crash down on top of me for several more seconds, showering me with broken glass.

The rats were screaming, and I may have been too—it all happened so quickly.

At last the lights and shelves stopped falling, and I uncurled a little. The rats were still squealing in terror at their fall, and for some time I lay on my back, dazed, wondering vaguely what had happened. My lab had fallen to pieces. Rat cages were all over the floor. I'd almost been killed.

I wormed my way out from under the debris, my eyes squinting in the faint light still emitted by the computer screen.

Then I noticed a crackling, sputtering sound, almost like corn popping in hot oil. I began to smell burned, or singed . . . something. Something like overdone pork chops. I couldn't tell what.

I peered around and saw a busted light fixture collapsed in a tangle of broken glass and loose wires over one of the rat cages. One of the loose wires was jumping, and throwing off tiny sparks on the wire cage. The motionless, lumpish shapes of three rats lay within.

The smell of singed rat hair poured into my nostrils and down into my lungs, and a bitter taste of bile gagged the back of my throat.

I shoved the smashed light fixture off the cage, receiving a brief, nasty shock on the side of my hand from the hot wire. I cried out at the pain, shaking my arm to ward off the numbness.

Kneeling in the dark, I opened the cage and gently lifted the rats one at a time and laid them on the worktable next to the computer.

Rats Eleven, Twelve, and Thirteen were dead.

After dragging a standing floor lamp from the big room out front and plugging it in, I spent the next several hours cleaning up the lab a little—righting all the knocked-over rat cages and sweeping up the broken glass.

None of the other rats had been seriously injured—they're tough little guys, and it takes more than a plunge off a wall to hurt them. But they were in a state of serious panic, and nothing I could do would calm them. Their constant pips and squeals were getting to me.

At first I couldn't figure out what had caused the shelves to collapse and the lights to come flying down off the ceiling. I'd put them up myself, and though I'm not exactly a master carpenter, as the B in freshman shop attested, I'm not totally incompetent either. And what kind of coincidence was it that everything would fall apart *at the same time*?

After a brief inspection of the disaster area, however, the answer was obvious. All but one of the screws in the mounting brackets of the top two shelves had been removed, and the two screws that remained had been stripped. It was amazing that the shelves had stayed up at all. And the moment I had touched them—*boom!* Down they went. The light fixture had been similarly rigged, its wires purposely frayed and exposed.

I'd been sabotaged. And there was only one person who could have done it—Hillis Milner.

I examined the three rats that had been electrocuted. Their white fur was branded with the diamond pattern of the wire cage like steaks on a grill. Electrocuted like condemned murderers.

I had been going to kill them anyway, but there was something about seeing those three dead rats that unhinged me. Maybe I was in a state of shock. I'd had enough adrenaline pumping to keep me relatively levelheaded for a while. But when I saw the burn marks on those rats, I just about lost it.

I didn't *like* having to kill rats—I never liked killing anything. Even when I was little, I didn't burn ants with a magnifying glass or pull the wings off flies the way other kids did.

Even knowing it was for a purpose, I could barely bring myself to execute the rats. But now I couldn't use these three in my experiment. They'd died for no reason. I was choking back anger in addition to disgust now.

But I wouldn't give Hillis the satisfaction. I wouldn't allow him the victory of murdering three of my rats and making them go to waste.

Normally I would have dissected the rats, bathed various organs—livers, kidneys, lungs, brains—in the protein solution, and then frozen them. After two days I would thaw the organs and determine how much the cells had deteriorated. But it was too late in the evening to dissect the three dead rats—I was bone tired and crazy with anger.

Crazy with anger.

Filling a syringe with a sample of the protein extract, I injected the serum directly into each rat and put their bodies back in their cage.

A small part of me knew it was pointless—you can't start changing procedures in the middle of an experiment and hope to learn anything.

So why did I do it? What was I thinking? What did I hope to prove?

Even now I ask myself these questions.

And only one answer comes rushing back to me: I wish to God I hadn't.

Six

◆

"I'm going to kill him," I concluded. I had just finished telling Gina and Ian about the previous night's events.

"Alec, don't do anything crazy," Gina pleaded. "Why don't you go to the police?"

"The police?" I snorted. "And what? Charge Hillis with attempted murder?"

"How about three counts of voluntary rodent-slaughter?" Ian suggested. Then, imitating Jimmy Cagney, he added, "You dirty rat."

"Very funny." I wasn't laughing.

"Negligent raticide?"

"Ha-ha, funnyman." I was in no mood for jokes, but Ian forced me to smile. "I'll tell you who's the dead duck, though—Hillis Milner."

We were leaning against Gina's Ford Escort. She drove Ian to school almost every morning. Like me, Ian had thought Hillis's threats were laughable, and he still wasn't able to take the situation completely seriously.

I could understand that. There was something so *dudish* about Hillis that it was hard even for me to stay angry at him for long. And of course I wasn't planning on literally killing Hillis—but putting him in a coma wasn't out of the question.

"Well, why don't you tell your boss at work about Hillis's messing with your stuff?" Gina asked.

"What do you think, Ian?" I said, ignoring Gina's suggestion. "A baseball bat to the knees or his head in a vise?"

"Both," he replied.

"Alec," Gina said, "I'm serious. There are better ways to get revenge than beating him up."

"Don't worry about it, Gina," I said. "I'm not really going to hurt him—just scare him a little. And you're right about work—when I tell the doctors at CytoTek about his little prank, they'll go nuts. He won't be allowed in the front door after this afternoon."

"Aw, c'mon, Alec," said Ian. "Can't we beat

him up a little? One broken bone is all I ask."

"You're awful." Gina grinned, and punched Ian's shoulder. Then the warning bell for first period rang.

"Hey, catch you later." I trotted off for class.

I hadn't seen Hillis around the grounds that morning, and when I asked a couple of kids if they knew where he was, they all said they hadn't seen him either.

At lunch Ruben Shiftman raised his eyebrows in surprise at my asking after Hillis. "So you decided to go out for the hundred after all, Baines? Milner said you'd wise up."

"Oh, I wised up all right," I said. "But I'm still not interested in that junk Hillis sells."

Ruben shrugged. "Whatever you say. But he wasn't in history this morning."

Hillis must have decided to be sick today. That was all right. He couldn't avoid me forever.

"Next time you see him, you tell Hillis that the next time *I* see him, I'm going to kick his butt."

"Sure, Baines. My pleasure. If I didn't, uh, need him, I'd do it myself." Ruben laughed, then regarded me thoughtfully. "I don't know what's going on here, but I'm surprised—why are you even bothering? I mean, geez, Baines, the guy's such a . . . such a . . ."

75

"Dude?"

"Yeah. The guy's such a dude. What'd he do to you? I mean, he's hardly worth the trouble of beating up."

Ruben was right, of course. But I still wanted Hillis to *think* I was going to trash him.

"Know what you mean." I got up from the lunch table. "But if you see him this weekend, give him the message."

"Hello, Alec. Come on in," Callie's mother called to me from the front doorway the next day. It was a sunny, warm Saturday afternoon. Halloween was only a week away, and yet the weather was still too warm for winter coats.

Mrs. Mitchell was in a plain blue-gingham housedress. Her short, graying hair was cut short. She stood with her hands on her hips, framed in the kitchen doorway as if she were posing for a full-length portrait.

"Hey, Mrs. M.," I called back as I jogged up to the house. Then I noticed Mr. Mitchell in the living room, watching the Washington-U.S.C. football game. "Hello, sir," I said politely.

"Hmph," he replied without looking up. He lifted his beer bottle in a vague gesture.

I liked talking to Mrs. Mitchell, and I could

tell she adored me, even if I was dating her daughter. But Mr. Mitchell was another story.

The first time I'd met him, he'd hardly said two words to me, and those two were gruff ones. It had been like that ever since. Sometimes I couldn't get more than a grunt out of him.

"Who's winning?" I asked him in a lame attempt to make conversation.

"Huskies, seven zip."

Three words! Three whole words! A new record! I turned to Mrs. Mitchell. "Where's Callie?"

"Upstairs, I think, getting dressed—off to a late start today."

"Not so late, Mom," Callie said, bouncing down the stairs. She had on jeans and a white sweatshirt with the sleeves torn off at the elbows. "So where to, Alec?" she said, snatching the Huskies cap from my head and putting it on her own.

"No plans. Figured we'd go for a drive, maybe into Seattle. I thought we'd go downtown, take a walk through the market."

"Ooh, I read there's a wonderful exhibit at the Art Institute on the history of dance photography," Mrs. Mitchell volunteered.

"Uh, gee, Mrs. M., that sounds real interesting," I said without much enthusiasm.

"Yes, you should see the—"

"Mom," Callie cut in. "I have a feeling Alec isn't dying to see the dance-photography show."

"Right. Well, you two have fun, wherever you're going. Drive carefully, Alec."

"I always do." Parents love it when you say things like that. "Good-bye, Mr. Mitchell."

Callie's dad lifted his beer bottle. "Nuh," he said.

When we were out the door, Callie said, "Sorry about the 'rents."

"It's fine, Callie. Your mom's nice, even if she doesn't have a clue about what teenagers like to do. I gotta admit, though, your dad's not exactly a barrel of laughs."

"He's coming around, Alec. The other day at dinner he even mentioned you by name."

"Great—my girlfriend's father hates me."

"He doesn't hate you. It's just that—you've got to give him another chance."

"Give him a chance? What about him giving me a chance? It's not like I've ever been rude or disrespectful to him, or gotten you pregnant or anything."

"No, you haven't, but you are my first serious boyfriend, you know."

"I am?"

"Of course, silly. Didn't you know that?"

No, actually, I hadn't. I'd sort of assumed that Callie had had boyfriends in Ohio before she moved out to Washington. I'd never asked about them, though. Better not to know, I figured.

"Sure. Of course I knew that," I said.

"Uh-huh," Callie replied. "Anyway, don't you see? You don't have to be rude for Dad to have a hard time with you. I'm his only daughter. Dad's very protective of me. He's been that way ever since . . ." She looked away.

"Ever since your sister died?"

"Yeah. Since Jessie died."

We were silent for a moment. Slipping the key into the ignition, I said, "I'll give him another chance. Everybody deserves two."

"I'd really appreciate that, Alec. He's a good guy. You'll see."

We were tooling along on one of the state highways outside of town, heading nowhere in particular. The towering, ancient fir trees speeding by in a blur threw their shadows across the road. The windshield flashed in and out of the sun like it was under a strobe lamp.

I was bringing Callie up-to-date on the Hillis situation. With all my running around in the morning and between classes searching for Hillis,

I hadn't had time even to say hello to Callie all day on Friday, and then she'd spent the evening with her family, celebrating her mother's birthday.

"So Hillis was 'sick' yesterday because he knew I'm going to wring his neck when I find him."

"I'm so sorry about your lab. And those poor little rats. It's all so gruesome." Callie sighed. "Have you done like Gina said and told the doctors at CytoTek what happened?"

"Nah. I haven't been back to CytoTek since Thursday night, when the accident happened."

"Alec! Turn the car around right now and let's go. You've got to fix the lab up again and get back to work on your experiment. The rats must be starving by now with no one to care for them."

"The rats are fine. They have enough food and water to last for three or four days at least. Although the bottoms of the cages might be getting pretty nasty by now," I added.

"Well, let's go, then."

"I don't have the heart for it, Cal. My experiment is ruined. Three of my rats were killed. I know I have to go back sometime, and I will . . . maybe tomorrow."

"Alec, turn the car around and let's go back to Ellswood. I'll help you clean up. I'm sure some of your work is salvageable. *Most* of the rats were fine—you said so yourself. And you still have your computer files and that fish oil, or whatever you call that stuff you were working with. If we're lucky, Hillis will be there, and I'll give him a karate chop of my own for good measure. Now let's get going."

"Okay." I smiled. "You're right. I can't put this off forever, and maybe my experiment isn't completely ruined."

Two of the doctors were in their offices when we got to CytoTek. Dr. Pensall heard us come in, and asked me to help her with the new copy machine. For some reason, she said, she couldn't get it to work properly. All she was getting out of it was blank sheets. When I pointed out to her that she was putting her originals on the glass faceup, she was exceedingly grateful.

All in a day's work at CytoTek.

Callie and I made our way back to my little wrecked laboratory broom closet, she stifling a snicker at helpless Dr. Pensall.

"Don't laugh," I said. "Dr. Pensall may not be able to use a Xerox machine, but she'll probably win the Nobel Prize for chemistry someday."

"I'm not laughing *at* her," Callie said, bursting into giggles. "Much."

"Here we are," I said, opening the door and clicking on the standing lamp I'd plugged in on Thursday night. The rats gave off their customary burst of pips at having their peace disturbed. They sounded a lot better, though, than they had two nights ago, when they were squealing in terror.

"Oh, Alec," Callie whispered. "I'm so sorry."

The lab was still a mess. Cages were piled on the floor and table. The fallen shelves were scattered across the room, and the shattered light fixture was heaped in the corner where I'd tossed it.

I stood in the doorway surveying the damage while Callie picked her way over the debris. She poked her finger into one of the cages on the worktable and made kissing noises at the rats inside.

I went out to the hallway and put my back against the wall, sinking slowly down till I was resting with my elbows on my knees. I rubbed the heels of my hands into my eyes and sighed a deep, long sigh.

"Alec?"

"Yeah?"

"I thought you said three of your rats had been killed."

"That's right. Killed, fried, barbecued."

"All the rats in here are alive."

"On the table," I said wearily. "You can't miss

82

them. They're the ones that aren't moving."

"Alec, I'm telling you, all the rats on the table are alive."

Groaning, I pushed myself slowly back up the wall and shuffled into the lab. "They're right over here, right where I left them on Thursday night." I pointed to a cage next to the computer.

In the cage were three breathing, scurrying, very much alive rats.

A feeling of raw iciness slid down my spine.

"I—I—put them right there." I approached the cage slowly. "I *think* I put them there."

When you've worked around as many rats as I have, you begin to be able to tell them apart. Even though they all have perfect, identical white fur and pink eyes, they're still individuals. Callie wouldn't have believed me, but I knew from the way they moved that rats Eleven, Twelve, and Thirteen were in that cage, looking as alive and healthy as they ever had. And there was one more thing—the diamond pattern of the wire cage seared into their fur.

"Maybe the cleaning people came in and moved things around," Callie said, stacking cages neatly along the back of the worktable. "Maybe they threw the dead ones out."

"The janitors know better than to mess with

the equipment, and they would *never* throw anything away without asking first."

"You must've been mistaken when you thought they were killed then," Callie said nonchalantly. "They were only stunned from the shock, and now they're okay again. That's great, isn't it?"

"Callie, those rats were dead. I'm sure of it." I was standing next to them, peering into their cage, but somehow I couldn't bring myself to touch them. Their little pink eyes stared back at me.

"Don't be silly, Alec." She turned to me, her hands on her hips. "It was late, the room was dark, you didn't examine them closely."

"But I did examine them. I can tell a dead rat from a live one, even one that's been knocked out."

"Alec, remember what you said to me? 'You have to look at it rationally.' Well, let's look at it rationally. Either these *are* the rats you thought were dead, and you were wrong. Or these *aren't* the rats you thought were dead, and someone did something with the dead ones. Dead is dead. Living things don't just come back."

Maybe not, I thought. Maybe they have to be brought back.

Seven

◆

Winter came late to western Washington that year. It was the end of October and warm enough, at least on sunny days, to wear shorts and a T-shirt, and I was still driving around with the top down on my Triumph.

The air tasted like winter, though—I could always smell road salt months before any was laid down. Ellswood had taken on that wary look that small towns get in autumn. The beaches at the lake were deserted, and the boats had been put into dry dock. I wasn't feeling that sense of wariness, however. My research at CytoTek was going well, school was a breeze, and best of all, Callie and I were more in love than ever.

With other girls, I had been bored on the second date and asleep by the end of the third. It seemed like I'd known Callie forever, even though it had been less than two months. At the same time, those two months had passed amazingly quickly. It seemed like it was only yesterday that we'd first kissed under the goalposts.

I'd memorized her every feature—the mole under her right eye, the lower-left canine tooth that was a little crooked. And yet I never grew tired of looking at her. On the few days when we didn't see each other, it was as if I was going without food and water.

What did she get in return? I wasn't sure. She jokingly pretended to be resigned to the idea that we were meant to be, that it was fate that had brought us together.

Fate.

I was willing to accept that. I had no choice but to.

"So where're we going?" Gina asked. It was early on the evening of October 31. I'd picked up Callie after school and swung by Ian's house, where he and Gina were waiting for me.

"Alec says it's a secret," Callie said, and tousled my hair. "He's being *very* mysterious."

Gina and Ian squeezed themselves into the tiny backseat of the Triumph. "I hope you know what you're doing, Alec," said Ian. "We're passing up Lori Fordham's five-kegger for your little secret, so it better be a good one."

"You'll find out where we're going," I said, pulling away from the curb, "when we get there."

The drive took us into some pretty desolate countryside. The outskirts of Ellswood don't peter out into newer, "planned" developments and neighborhoods, the way a lot of towns do. When you reach Ellswood's city limits, you know it.

One minute you're driving along a road lined with shade trees and houses, and the next minute the town drops away, and disappears into a dense forest. And that's it—just the brick-red trunks of trees against the dark-green slopes of hills, the occasional abandoned logging trail, and the silence of mile after mile of hemlock and fir.

After a few minutes I turned off the state highway and onto a dirt road that didn't even have a county number. It cut straight up and down the hills, turning at right angles rather than curving through the valleys the way the highway did. Even weighted down with four people, my old Triumph could top out pretty well on the crests of the hills, and Callie, Ian, and Gina screamed and clutched their stomachs every time we flew over one. In the gathering darkness I was lucky to spot the unmarked turnoff I'd been watching for.

The road was in such poor shape, I eventually had to slow down to second gear, but still the low-slung Triumph kept bottoming out. Overgrown bushes and tall grass lashed the sides of the car. Out of the vegetation on the right emerged one of those large gray electrical towers that look like Erector Set giants relaying power lines through the forest.

"Hey, Alec," Ian called. "I didn't know you were going to be taking us through the jungle." He ducked a branch. "Maybe we should put the top back on before we get our heads ripped off."

"No need. We're almost there."

"And where is 'there,' Alec?" Gina asked.

"'There' is here," I answered as the road suddenly ended in a broad, open field. I cut the engine and we glided silently to a halt at the edge of the grass.

About a hundred yards away, the black silhouette of a farmhouse rose against the red of the western sky. A cicada trilled in the distance and was interrupted by the cry of a nearby crow.

"Happy Halloween, boys and girls," I said, rolling my eyes back and wringing my hands. "Welcome to the house of horrors." I cackled until Gina slapped me gently upside the head.

"You're insane, Alec," she said.

"Yes. *Criminally*."

"Who lives here?" Callie whispered.

"No one," I said, unlatching the door, "except maybe a few ghosts. Come on, check it out." I went around to the back of the Triumph and popped the trunk. Inside was a small wicker hamper, which I'd packed with fried chicken, potato chips, pretzels, and a twelve-pack of beer.

Ian and Gina pried themselves out of the backseat and clambered over the sides of the car.

"Eats! Brew!" said Ian, geeing the picnic basket and beer. "All right! I've forgotten Lori's party already."

"Down, boy," I said, tucking the beer under an arm and grabbing a basket handle. "Get the other end of this, would ya?"

"Yes sir, yes sir."

"You coming, Callie?" Gina asked.

Callie hadn't stirred since we'd pulled into

the field. "Yeah. Yeah, sure, I'm coming," she said, not moving an inch.

To the left of the house was a small, brackish reservoir. It was about sixty feet from bank to bank and almost perfectly circular. The water was a dark brownish-green, and a thick layer of bright-green scum covered much of the surface. It was impossible to tell how deep the water was. But judging from the large mound of dirt piled near the bank opposite the road, someone had dug a pretty ambitious hole.

On the side opposite where we stood a single rotting pier jutted almost to the center of the reservoir, the pilings disappearing into the murky water after only a couple of inches. Though there was a slight, steady breeze, no waves lapped the slimy banks. And there was no sign of any fish or frogs or turtles or ducks, or any other creature you'd normally expect to find living in a pond. The water was so choked with algae that nothing else could survive. Swirling clouds of gnats hovered above the surface.

"Ooh, that water looks so inviting, Ian," Gina said brightly. "Let's go swimming right away."

"Mmm-*mmm*," he said, smacking his lips.

"Sounds enticing. Unfortunately, I forgot my bathing suit."

"We can go skinny-dipping, then!" she said. "Alec, you go first."

"So kind of you to offer, Gina. Maybe later. Come on, Ian, let's drag this stuff up on the porch before I decide to throw your girlfriend in the water."

We started up to the house.

"Alec, wait up," Callie said, tugging on my elbow. She had rushed up from the car and was breathing heavily. "I don't want to go in there. It gives me the creeps."

"It's supposed to give you the creeps, Callie. Tonight's Halloween."

"I mean it, Alec. I don't like this place." Callie gripped my arm tightly. "Are you sure no one lives here?"

"Callie, I've been here before," I explained. "Believe me, no one lives here."

She smiled halfheartedly and nodded toward the house, dropping her hand from my arm. "Maybe it's Halloween getting to me."

The four of us stopped and looked the house over.

It *was* spooky—which was precisely the reason I'd chosen it as the site of my surprise

91

Halloween party. It was a simple, two-story wooden structure. The rotting front porch sagged on low concrete stilts. The outside hadn't been painted in decades, and the wood had weathered to a uniform tombstone gray. Most of the windows had been busted, though there were still wavy panes in several of the ones upstairs.

Scattered about in front were pieces of old farm implements and broken appliances—an ancient washing machine, a rusty-orange tiller—along with other bits of junk—empty oilcans and pint whiskey bottles, a couple of hubcaps and some spent shotgun shells. It was a desolate, lonely place—perfect for all Hallows' Eve.

"How did you find this old place out in the middle of nowhere?" Gina asked me as we climbed up onto the porch.

I stared into the middle distance and spoke in a monotone. "I was brought here by the living dead. . . ."

"Alec!" Callie said. "That's not funny."

"Sorry. Actually, we're really not that far from town. About a mile over that way"—I gestured toward the back of the house—"is the Burlington Trail."

"Really?" Ian said. "It seemed like we drove

pretty far. That backseat is a killer."

"You have to take a roundabout route to get here by car," I said, ignoring his complaint. "I found it a couple of weeks ago when I was running on the Trail. Thanks to Callie"—I gave her a nudge—"I hadn't gone running in a while. After about two miles I was so pooped, I had to stop and take a breather. Then I noticed a bunch of raspberry bushes growing by the side of the trail. And since I was getting hungry, too. . . . Anyway, I followed them up the bank—"

"And ate your way here," Gina finished for me.

"Something like that. It's pretty amazing—there's a huge raspberry patch that comes right up to the back door. It's got to be at least ten acres. It's completely overgrown. I guess the people here used to be berry farmers."

The front door was unlocked, but its hinges were rusted solid. The first time I'd been to the house, I'd climbed in through a front window. This time Ian and I applied our shoulders to the door and forced it open.

The house was as spooky inside as out. Debris—old magazines, a child's doll with no head, some shattered plates—was scattered all over the floor, as were various pieces of junky old furniture. Several generations of wallpaper—a plain gray over a floral pattern over a blue-and-white stripe—were curling off the walls. In the room to the left, which I guess had been a sort of parlor, was a large stone fireplace. To the right was a smaller room and a narrow staircase, which led to the second floor. Behind the smaller room was the kitchen.

The wildlife that would not live in the reservoir seemed to have moved into the house. As Ian and I burst through the front door, I saw a rat—and not one of the nice clean white ones of the lab, but a big brown ugly one—scurrying toward the kitchen. There were spiderwebs in the corners of the ceiling. In the failing light, it was hard to see the spiders themselves, but their white egg sacs shone clearly enough.

"Ooo-ooo-ooh," Ian moaned like a ghost. Then he said, "I'm going exploring," popped open a beer, and started up the stairs.

"Be careful," Gina called after him. "All I need is for him to step on a nail up there," she muttered to Callie. Then, "Hey, are you all right?"

Callie was standing in the doorway. She was running her hands through her hair over and over. "I—I'm fine," she said.

"Why don't you come sit down," I said. A wooden stool lay on its side near the fireplace. I set it upright and dusted it off with my hand. "Here."

Callie sat on the stool, and immediately bent over and started massaging her temples. "I have a bit of a headache," she said.

I rubbed the back of her neck and glanced at Gina, who shrugged.

"I'll take care of Callie," Gina offered. "You go make sure my boyfriend doesn't fall through a rotten floorboard or something."

I headed up the stairs, but before I was up three steps, a sound came to me that froze me in place.

Callie was moaning now, and not jokingly, as Ian had earlier. She was sobbing into her hands, as if she was in real pain. I rushed back down the stairs. Gina was standing next to her, looking stricken. She put her hand on Callie's shoulder.

"Don't touch me!" Callie spat out, flinging Gina's hand away with her arm.

"Sorry!" Gina said, making a face. "I was just trying to—"

"Get away from me!"

Gina backed away a few paces. I darted to

Callie and knelt beside her, trying to draw her hands from her face. "Callie, what's wrong? Are you sick?"

She brushed me away and cried, "No, no, I'm fine! Leave me alone. Just leave me alone."

She was hunched on the low stool, rocking back and forth, wiping her eyes and cheeks with the palms of her hands. Her hair was matted in a damp tangle around her face. Her arms were wet with tears, and she couldn't stop the sobbing.

I moved to hold her, but she shoved me away. "Get away from me!" she screamed, hysterical now. "Get away from me!"

"Callie! What's the matter with you?"

"Nothing's the matter with me!" she shouted through clenched teeth, trying to regain control of herself. "It's nothing. It's just—just—I'm scared, Alec. I'm so scared. And I hate this place." She dropped her hands into her lap and looked up at me. Her eyes were bloodshot, and her nose and lips were swollen from crying.

"What are you afraid of, Callie?"

"Oh, Alec, can't you feel it?" she asked bitterly. "Can't you feel it at all?"

"Feel what? It's just an old house." I gestured to the room around us. Sure, the house was spooky, but it wasn't *that* terrifying. "What are you so upset about?"

"It's *not* just an old house, Alec. There's something—something here. Something—I'm scared, Alec. I'm so scared. I feel like something horrible is going to—I feel it's—It's—" Callie seemed confused, as if she were talking to herself, trying to work something out. She was heaving violently, as if she was about to hyperventilate. Then at once she became calmer, as though she'd come to a sudden realization.

"It feels like the end of everything, Alec. The end of *everything*. This house stinks of death. Can't you smell it? It reeks of death." She was getting hysterical again. "It's all through this place—all around us. It's inside us. Oh, Alec, I hate this—"

She glared at me accusingly. "I told you I hated this place! I told you, but you made me come here. You made me come here anyway!"

"Callie, what are you talking about? Gina, what is she talking about?"

"Alec," Gina said, "Callie's upset. Maybe we should get going."

"But what about all the food I packed?"

"Alec!" Gina shot her eyes toward Callie, who now was slumped over, weeping quietly.

"You're right," I said. "You take Callie back to the car. Ian and I'll carry the stuff."

Callie allowed Gina to lead her to the car, and I explained the situation to Ian. We drove home without any of us saying another word. Callie was still crying when I dropped her off at her house.

Eight

◆

About a week after the stunt with the shelves, Ian and I finally caught up with Hillis in the hallway at school between fifth and sixth periods. He of course denied knowing anything about what had happened at CytoTek.

"And I suppose you were never even *in* my lab," I said.

"That's right," Hillis said. He shifted his weight from foot to foot. "I never went near it." He sniffed loudly and gave a little cough. "I've had the flu for a week. That's why I've been out of school." He coughed again. "See?"

"Uh-huh," Ian muttered.

I took a step toward Hillis.

"Hey, man, take it easy," he said. "Take it easy. You weren't hurt, and neither were your lousy rats."

I took another step toward him.

"Take it easy," he repeated. "Hey." He tossed the hair out of his eyes. "Take it easy, man."

"Hillis, I don't want to fight you," I said. "I really don't. You're liable to bleed all over me."

Ian snickered.

"But if you ever do anything like that again, I'll cut your heart out. And don't think you can get Ruben Shiftman to protect you. He doesn't like you any more than I do. So do everyone a favor and behave, okay?" I clapped him on the shoulder and leered.

"Okay, man. Okay." He scurried down the hall, calling over his shoulder, "Take it easy."

"Do you think it sank in?" Ian asked quietly, watching Hillis's lanky form disappear into a crowd of students.

"Who knows?"

Thanks to Hillis's prank, I was onto something important with the rats. I didn't want anyone—not Hillis, not the janitors, not the doctors—nosing around my lab. I wanted to keep as low a profile at CytoTek as possible, so I'd decided not to tell anyone that Hillis had sabotaged my lab. Especially since I couldn't prove it anyway.

"Who knows?" I repeated to Ian. "But who really cares?"

As far as I was concerned, the matter was closed.

Dr. Pensall was bent over a microscope, adjusting the lens with one hand while taking notes with the other.

"Where will you be going to school next year, Alec?" she asked without looking up.

She was a stout, middle-aged woman with straight, dirty-blond hair that she kept tied back in a ponytail. I suspected she looked exactly the same when she'd gone to college, back in the sixties. "Johns Hopkins or Cal Tech?"

"I'm not sure." I was prepping some slides in her lab at CytoTek. "Actually, I was thinking maybe I'd stay in state. Washington has a great bio department, you know."

Dr. Pensall sat back and rubbed her eyes. "True, it does. Still, you can't beat Johns Hopkins."

"It's pretty far away, though."

"What about Cal Tech, then? Southern California, you know—not that far from home. And it's beautiful. Sun all the time, even when it's smoggy. I'm from Pomona myself."

"Huh."

"You don't sound too thrilled by the idea of Cal Tech." Dr. Pensall eyed me skeptically.

"I sort of prefer U.W., that's all."

"It's the money, isn't it?"

"Well, staying in state would knock about fifty grand off my loans. That's something to consider."

"Look, Alec, I did graduate work at Cal Tech. I know people in admissions, financial aid. You can get scholarships, work-study, grants, you name it." She leaned back over her microscope and started scribbling in a log. "I'd be glad to help you out with a recommendation."

"Thanks, Dr. Pensall. I'll think about it."

"Do. Meantime, tell me about the work you're doing here. Your lab looks like a disaster area." Her pen scratched away. It was amazing how she could look through a microscope, take notes on what she was seeing, and carry on a conversation all at the same time.

"I had a little accident. Some shelves fell. No big deal."

"Uh-huh. And what are you working on?"

"Nothing too interesting. Organic tissue-preservation techniques."

"Cold-water fish proteins?"

"Yeah. Newfoundland ocean pout."

"Interesting. Ion balance improved?"

"Yeah." I was impressed. This wasn't even her field, and she really kept up. "I've had a couple of big surprises lately."

"Good surprises, I hope."

I was tempted to tell her all about the rats' coming back to life. But somehow I couldn't bring myself to do it. "Yeah. Real good."

"Great." Her hand never stopped writing down notes on what she saw through the microscope. "And what is Hillis working on?" She asked it casually, but I detected a slight change in her tone of voice.

"I'm not sure."

"Some of his rats have serious weight problems," Dr. Pensall commented.

"Yeah, I noticed that too."

"Older boys—athletes—sometimes come by here for Hillis," she said. "Do you know anything about that?" She didn't look up, but her hand stopped moving.

"I guess he has friends at Anselm," I said cagily. I still didn't want to fink on Hillis, despite what Gina had said.

"You know, if he's doing anything illegal

here, we could all be in a great deal of trouble."

"Yes, ma'am."

"And he hasn't told you what he's up to?"

"No, ma'am."

Dr. Pensall leaned back from her microscope. "Tomorrow, when Hillis comes in, I'm going to ask him what he's working on and to show me the documentation. If his answer isn't satisfactory, I'm going to fire him."

"I see."

"I'll also have to ask him if anyone else at CytoTek knew what he was working on."

I didn't say anything. All I could do if Hillis decided to drag me down with him was deny it.

"So I'm going to ask you again, Alec. Do you know what he's working on?"

"I can't say I haven't had suspicions." I gazed at her levelly. "But I've never discussed Hillis's experiment with him."

Dr. Pensall studied me for a long moment. "Good. I believe you haven't." Without another word, she leaned back over her microscope and resumed her note taking.

I was cruising the halls at school two days later when Hillis accused me of ratting on him.

"I don't know what you're talking about," I said.

"Pensall fired me last night, man," Hillis said.

Ruben Shiftman was standing behind him, flexing the muscles in his neck threateningly. What a load.

"So you got fired?" I said. "Tough. What do you want me to do about it?"

"I want you to . . . to . . ." Hillis was at a loss.

Ruben stepped forward. "I think you told somebody something you shouldn't've. I think you're out to get Hillis."

"I couldn't care less about Hillis or what you think."

"You told me yourself you were going to kick his butt. I think you decided to get him an easier way."

"Kicking his ass would've been the easiest thing I could've done," I challenged. "But I decided not to. As far as I'm concerned, it's over."

"Not over yet, pretty boy," Ruben said, shoving me in the chest with both hands.

"Yeah, pretty boy," Hillis echoed.

"Shut up, goofball," I snapped at Hillis. Then, to Ruben, "What do you care about this dude, anyway?" I knew the answer already, though. Ruben was pissed because Hillis no longer had a lab. And no lab meant no "performance boosters."

"Hillis is a friend of mine," Ruben said.

"Then do him a favor and tell him to get lost." I took a step toward Ruben. "What, afraid to lose the steroids he's been selling you? Is that what you're so worked up about? Won't be able to make it through football practice without them?" I smiled.

Ruben took a swing at me.

I knew it was coming and pulled back just in time, counterpunching with a jab to his nose. It didn't hurt him, but it did take him by surprise. He stood with a puzzled look on his face. I waited for him to come at me again. This time I probably wouldn't come out of it so well. Ruben was strong enough and tough enough to take me.

He hesitated.

"Go, man," Hillis muttered, shoving him forward a little.

Ruben glanced over his shoulder at Hillis, and I took the opportunity, letting fly with a right hand that smacked against his temple and sent him stumbling into the lockers that lined the wall. It was a sucker punch, sure. But on the other hand, Ruben had tried to sucker-punch me.

Hillis gaped as Ruben leaned against the lockers, shaking his head to clear it. Hillis met my eye.

"Hey, man," he said, holding up his hands and backing off.

Next thing I knew Ruben had his arms locked around me and was driving me into the lockers on the other side of the hallway. A locker handle dug into the small of my back, and I yelped in pain. I clamped Ruben's head under my arm and tried to bash it into the locker handle, but his leverage was better than mine, and we sort of spun-slid in a circle for several seconds before someone started prying us apart.

It was Mr. Beerman, the same teacher who'd broken up the fight with Hillis. "Boys, boys!" he was shouting. "Boys! Settle down." He held Ruben and me apart with his arms extended. "What's going on here?"

"Nothing," Ruben muttered.

"Yeah, nothing," I said also.

"It looked like more than nothing to me," Mr. Beerman observed. He was a regular Einstein.

"It was nothing really," Ruben said.

"Just a little difference of opinion," I added.

"Just a little difference of opinion, eh?" Mr. Beerman asked.

Ruben and I nodded miserably.

"Then why don't you boys shake hands and put it behind you?"

We grunted our assent. Mr. Beerman was still holding us apart. His pants were drooping dangerously low. We reached across him and shook hands, each gripping as hard as he could in an effort to break the other's fingers.

"There." Mr. Beerman beamed. "Friends again." And this moron taught psychology. "Next time I catch either one of you making trouble, it's straight to the principal. And you know Mr. Gurties. He likes to run a *tight ship*. Now clear out and don't be late to your next class."

Finally he released us. Glaring at each other, we headed in opposite directions. Hillis had long ago beat it.

I knew I hadn't seen the last of either of them.

Callie and I double-dated with Gina and Ian to Homecoming. We were playing the Rindell Eagles, our cross-county rivals. It was a fairly decent contest—at halftime we were leading seven to nothing on a rollout that Ruben had taken in for a score. Callie, Ian, Gina, and I were sitting where the crowd noise wasn't so deafening—at the top of the bleachers, near the twenty-yard line.

"Have you seen any of the floats?" Gina shouted to me above the roar of the crowd as the players trotted off the field at the end of the first half. She was wearing a pink beret.

"No!" I hollered back. I had my arm around Callie, and squeezed her shoulder. "Been too busy to check 'em out."

"I went over to Lori Fordham's to take a look at ours," Ian volunteered. As well as being senior-class treasurer and Homecoming Queen, Lori Fordham was in charge of the float committee. "They still hadn't settled on an idea. That was less than two weeks ago."

Homecoming theme this year was "Hooray for Hollywood!" The class floats were supposed to depict scenes from famous movies, with an Ellswood twist. Every year the freshman and sophomore classes, who make a float together, get first dibs on ideas—otherwise they might not be able to come up with anything at all. The junior class submits its idea next. Then the senior class has to work with whatever's left over.

"Lori's such a ditz," Gina said, screwing up her face. "I wonder if they got it built in time. It would be pretty embarrassing if we didn't enter a float at all."

"I'm sure we'll enter *something*," I said. "Lori's not that big of an airhead."

"Maybe *you* don't think so," Gina replied.

Callie looked back and forth between me and Gina but said nothing.

"Oh, we're entering something," Ian said.

"Yeah? What is it?" I asked.

"Don't know," Ian said. "But I heard Hillis worked on it."

"Hillis?" I was surprised. "I didn't think he'd be allowed on the committee. Hillis isn't exactly Lori's type. Isn't the float more a jock-prep thing?"

"I guess they were pretty desperate for ideas," Ian said. "Besides, Ruben wanted him on the committee."

"Ruben? Why?"

"Beats me." Ian shrugged. "But supposedly he and Hillis took over the whole committee and made them go with their idea. It helped that Lori has a crush on Ruben."

"Yeech," Gina said. "I told you she was a ditz."

I didn't reply.

"The idea they finally settled on was real top

110

secret," Ian continued. "Wouldn't tell anyone outside the committee what they were doing. Claimed they didn't want the other classes to steal their idea."

"Even though the other classes already had their ideas," I said.

"Yeah."

"So I wonder why it was such a big secret. . . ."

"Hey!" Callie said, pointing. She had been oddly quiet all evening. "Here comes the first float." The freshman-sophomore float led the parade, entering the stadium from the end zone near where we sat.

The "froshmore" float was a takeoff on *Jurassic Park*. A *Tyrannosaurus rex* in an Ellswood football uniform had a Rindell Eagle in its mouth. Across the base of the flatbed a banner said ELLSWOOD CHOMPS RINDELL. You had to hand it to them. It wasn't bad, for a bunch of froshes and sophs.

The junior float came next in the parade. It showed a ten-foot Batman holding a trident—we were the Ellswood Tridents—over a fallen Penguin whose face was made to look like a Rindell Eagle. A banner said GO TRIDENTS. It was kind of lame.

It wasn't nearly as stupid as the senior float,

111

however. When it pulled onto the track that circled the football field, the crowd started whispering, trying to figure out what the point of it was. Instead of being on a flatbed, like the freshman-sophomore and junior floats, it was on an old wooden hay wagon pulled by a pickup truck. It didn't seem to be a scene from any movie. The painted-canvas backdrop was a view of the famous "Hollywood" sign on the hills outside L.A. In the foreground was a movie theater, obviously made out of a refrigerator box. The marquee read "Hooray for Hollywood!" Next to the theater was the figure, about a foot or so tall, of a woman in a white dress. The whole thing was kind of dinky—it looked more like the set to a bad puppet show than a Homecoming float. Why had Hillis and Ruben insisted on keeping this ridiculous thing secret?

Following the senior float came Lori Fordham, Homecoming Queen, riding in a convertible Cadillac, waving condescendingly at her subjects. By the time the senior float had reached the fifty-yard line, the crowd was jeering and booing it. Lori had a stricken look on her face. She must have thought the boos were aimed at her.

"What is it?" Ian asked, meaning the float. "I don't get it."

"It doesn't have anything to do with Ellswood or Rindell," Gina said. "That Lori Fordham is a total ditz."

"I don't think it's Lori Fordham who's to blame," Callie muttered. I glanced over at her. In the artificial light of the football field, she looked pale, washed out. I could feel her body tensing up under my arm.

"What do you mean?" I asked her, but before the question was out of my mouth, I knew the answer.

I looked at the float: the Hollywood sign, the theater marquee, the girl in white. Hillis Milner had once mentioned that he knew why Callie's family had moved to Ellswood. The float reproduced the circumstances of Jessie's death exactly. It couldn't be a coincidence.

Suddenly a small object—a bottle or something—hurtled out of the crowd, trailing a thin line of smoke. When the bottle hit the float, it exploded in a ball of orange fire. The cardboard figures, the cloth backdrop, the wooden hay wagon were immediately engulfed in flames.

Lori Fordham really looked stricken now. It was a few moments before the driver of the pickup realized the float was on fire. When he did, he stopped, jumped out quick, and ran for it. I guess he didn't want to be around if the fire spread to the pickup's gas tank. Lori hopped off the Caddy and raced after him, her tiara falling onto the turf.

There was a lot of shouting in the crowd, and everyone was milling around excitedly, talking and pointing. Some were even laughing. It was pandemonium. At the bottom of the bleachers, near midfield, a dark figure in an overcoat loped through the crowd toward the far end zone, bobbing and lurching erratically as if he wanted to get away from there as fast as possible. As if he didn't want to be seen anywhere near the float.

I recognized that peculiar loping gait. But even if I hadn't seen him, I would have known it was Hillis Milner who'd tossed the firebomb.

Ian and Gina were staring in fascinated amusement at the scene down below. Neither Callie nor I had ever told them the story of Jessie's death. Like everyone else in the crowd, they didn't understand what was really going on—Ruben and Hillis had set the whole thing up to get at Callie and, through her, me.

By now a fire engine had entered the stadium and was parked right on the fifty-yard line. It was spraying water all over the charred hay wagon. So much for playing conditions in the second half. There was smoke all over the place, and it was getting difficult to see the field from where we were.

Then I realized Callie was no longer at my side. I spotted her making her way down the bleachers.

"Catch you later, guys." Waving at Gina and Ian, I bounded after Callie. They were so engrossed by the spectacle on the field, they hardly looked over to wave back.

I caught up with Callie in the parking lot.

"Callie." She was standing next to the Triumph. There was no other way for her to get home.

"Let's get out of here," she said. She was surprisingly calm. I had expected her to be upset, to say the least, over what Hillis and Ruben had done to her. I looked at her closely. She seemed fine.

"Right." I unlocked the doors, and we climbed in. I felt I had to say something. "Those dirtbags—"

"Don't," Callie said impatiently. "Let's not even talk about it."

I sat silently, not putting the key in the ignition.

At last Callie said, "Poor Lori Fordham.

Sure ruined her big night, didn't they?"

"Yeah," I agreed.

"You know, I'm not going to forget this," Callie said. "And I'm not going to let them get away with it, either." In her voice was something I'd never heard before—a coldness, a stoniness. A deadly seriousness. "I'll get them back, both of them. If it takes till the day I die, I'm going to make them pay."

I looked over at her, and she met my glance. There was in Callie's pretty green eyes a look of bitterness. Of hatred. Almost, I would say, of evil.

Nine

◆

It was noon on Christmas Eve already and I'd barely noticed it coming. I was too busy working with my rats to pay attention to anything so trivial as a holiday. Even this morning I'd gone in to CytoTek for a couple of hours, trying to get some work in before it locked up for the week.

Too busy working. That's how I described it. Obsessed is what Ian and Gina called me. It was true, I suppose. I was obsessed.

And the holidays were approaching fast.

Luckily, the Muzaked carols piped into the elevator at CytoTek, along with the blue aluminum tree that sprouted in the RoboCop Building's lobby a few days earlier, had invaded my consciousness long enough to remind me to get a present for Callie. The problem was: What to get her?

Due to the high cost of my wild lifestyle—meaning I ate at McDonald's once a week—and the low wage I earned at CytoTek, my bank account was not exactly bulging. So pearls, diamonds, and expensive perfume were out of the question.

But what else does a guy get his girlfriend for Christmas?

I considered going the inexpensive-but-heartfelt route and making her something. But what? I couldn't make anything nice—not even a pigeon or crow would live in the birdhouse I hammered together in freshman shop.

Maybe I could get her something cute, like a teddy bear. No. Callie would hate that. A CD or a book? Not romantic enough. If I knew how to knit, I said to myself, I could make her a sweater. Right. And if I knew how to spin straw into gold, I'd be a millionaire. . . .

It was Christmas Eve, and I still didn't have a present for Callie.

And we were getting together that night.

Time to panic.

Then I had a brilliant idea. Callie had given

me all those incredible photographs, which were lying in piles in my sock drawer at home. I must have had twenty or thirty great pictures of me, plus half a dozen or so good ones of Callie that I'd lucked out on. I'd make a collage out of the photos of our fall together, then buy a frame for it—a project that was not beyond my limited time, artistic abilities, and expense account.

Going through the picture collection, I selected nine shots of Callie (all the others were out of focus), twelve of myself (discarding another ten that were perfectly good), five of us together (taken by Ian or Gina), and ten of various places we'd been together, such as the Burlington Trail and the fish market in downtown Seattle. It was enough to make a decent-size collage, and by artfully arranging Callie's pictures toward the center and mine at the edges, I was able to make it less obvious that there weren't as many good shots of her.

I was pretty pleased with the result. And Callie would love it as a Christmas present.

"Hello?" I answered the phone.

"Hey, what's up?" It was Ian. He always started off his calls to me the same way.

"Nothing much, man, nothing much," I

replied, as always. "What's up with you?"

"Nothing much." The ritual complete, Ian began the conversation in earnest. "Hey, did you ever figure out what to do about Callie's Christmas present?"

"They don't call me boy genius for nothing, my friend," I replied, tying the bow on the gift-wrapped package. It was six o'clock. I'd be driving over to the RoboCop Building in half an hour to pick up some equipment before CytoTek closed for the holidays, then straight to Callie's from there.

I proceeded to tell Ian about the collage I'd made. He was suitably impressed.

"She's going to love that. You are a genius," he admitted.

"And what are you giving Gina?"

"Let's put it this way," he said. "I'm on my way to the mall now."

"Ouch." I could definitely sympathize with Ian's last-minute trip.

"Yeah, I didn't exactly plan in advance."

"Good luck."

"Well, merry Christmas," Ian said cheerfully.

"Happy holidays." We hung up.

I patted Callie's present affectionately, then went to change for dinner. For once, I was going to look marginally better than grungy.

"Merry Christmas, Alec." Callie's mom stood with her arms extended in the foyer of her house. Directly above her, suspended from a small chandelier, was a sprig of mistletoe.

"Merry Christmas, Mrs. M." I stepped forward and gave her a peck on the cheek. "This is for you and Mr. Mitchell." I handed her a box of cookies my mother had baked. "Pecan sandies."

"Why, thank you, Alec," she said. "That's very thoughtful of you."

"Actually, it was very thoughtful of my mother. It was her idea."

Mrs. Mitchell laughed. "Well, at least you're honest. And don't you look festive tonight."

I stroked my red-and-green striped tie. "Christmasy, eh?"

"Very handsome. Now let me go see what Callie is up to. She got back about fifteen minutes ago—she'd been out all day. . . . Jim," she called to her husband, "come see what Alec brought us for Christmas." She turned and left the foyer, humming "Deck the Halls."

In a moment Mr. Mitchell came striding up, arms out. I looked up, saw the mistletoe hanging above me, and scurried forward fast, grasping his hand in a firm handshake.

"Merry Christmas, sir."

"Merry Christmas, Alec!" Mr. Mitchell said with what seemed to be sincere heartiness. "Come sit down."

Six words! Well. 'Tis the season, and all that.

Just then Callie came bounding down from upstairs, clutching a large, brightly wrapped present. "Let's go, Alec. Time's awastin'!"

"What's the hurry, darling?" Mr. Mitchell asked. "Alec was about to sit down and have an eggnog with me."

I was?

But Callie wouldn't be slowed. "We've got places to go, people to see, presents to exchange." She hooked her elbow around mine and started dragging me to the door.

"Right," I said. I considered stopping her underneath the mistletoe, but then thought better of it. It looked like Mr. Mitchell might be coming around, and I didn't want to do anything that would set him against me again.

"Merry Christmas!" I shouted as Callie slammed the door behind us.

"Let's go," Callie said.

"So what *is* the hurry?"

"Can I throw this in the trunk?" Callie

asked, holding up her package.

"Sorry, full. Toss it in the back." Callie shoved the package into the tiny backseat, next to the one I had wrapped for her. "And what's with all the secrecy?" I asked.

For days she had been hinting about what she had planned for Christmas Eve. I had wanted to take her out somewhere for dinner, but she wouldn't hear of it. She had her own plans for us, she said. It was going to be part of my present.

"It's a mystery," she said. "A surprise." She leaned over and planted a warm kiss on my lips. "Now start 'er up and go where I tell you to," she commanded.

"Aye, aye, Cap'n."

It was finally beginning to feel like winter. I'd put the top on the Triumph the week before, and I was glad of it now. A light sleety rain was beginning to come down, the pellets rushing at my headlights as we drove through town.

"Your dad seemed friendlier tonight," I said.

"Oh?"

"Uh-huh."

After a few seconds Callie said, "Huh."

I waited for her to comment further on this development. She didn't.

"I was wondering if you might have had a little talk with him like you had with me," I said.

"I might have," she replied.

"I thought so. Well, as long as he doesn't hate me, I don't care—"

"Oops, take a left here." Callie gestured toward a darkened turnoff.

It was the old dirt road that led to the farmhouse where we'd had our Halloween party. Or rather, tried to have our Halloween party.

"Are you sure this is the way?" I asked.

"Sure I'm sure," she said.

The road was slick with the falling rain, which was sleetier now and heavier. The Triumph's tail kept fishtailing, and I had to struggle to keep it straight. The little sports car wasn't designed to go off-road, especially through icy mud.

"We haven't seen as much of each other lately," said Callie.

"I know," I said. "The lab has been taking up a lot of my time."

"You don't need to make excuses. I understand."

"Thanks. It's just that I . . . I think I'm onto something really significant."

"That's wonderful, Alec." I glanced over at

her and caught her glancing over at me. "Can you tell me what it is?"

"Of course. It has to do with that experiment in tissue preservation I told you about. . . . I'm having some real success with it."

"Oh." She could tell I wasn't telling her all I could.

The truth was that I was afraid—or was it ashamed?—to tell her what I was working on.

The three rats *had* been killed the night of the accident at CytoTek. I was sure of it. And—somehow—they had been revived by the protein extract I had injected into them.

For two months I had been working feverishly, trying to gain the secret of the reanimating solution—as I now was referring to it.

The night Hillis had sabotaged me, the three rats had been killed by an electric current from a light fixture. The usual method of killing rats—bashing their skulls in—would not allow for much chance of reanimation. I had to reproduce the circumstance of death of those first three rats.

So, using a small electric stove I'd borrowed from the kitchen at CytoTek and rewired, I rigged up what can only be described as an electric chair for rats.

There I'd execute them, watching as they struggled and jerked with the current, until finally they moved no more—until they were dead. Then I'd inject them with the reanimating solution and await the results.

Depending on the voltage used to electrocute them, the time elapsed during which they were dead, and the amount of reanimating solution injected into them, the rats took anywhere from two to four hours to revive. About half of them didn't revive at all.

Some, after coming back, died again in a few hours. The ones that lived—including the first three, numbers Eleven, Twelve, and Thirteen, who still bore the diamond brands of their execution—were . . . it's hard to say, exactly. There was something *different* about them. Nothing that could be quantified or counted. Just a feeling I got.

I hadn't told anyone at CytoTek about what I was doing. The doctors there had never really taken my work seriously—I was a kid. How could I tell them I'd discovered—stumbled upon, actually—something that scientists and philosophers alike had only dreamed about? Nature's most closely guarded treasure . . . the secret of life.

I'd tried to tell Dr. Pensall about it. She treated me more like a colleague—less like a gofer—than the other doctors did. But I couldn't bring myself to say to her, "Gee, Doc, I have this problem. I've been killing rats and bringing them back to life. What should I do now?"

Scientific research was a cutthroat business. I was afraid that my discovery would be taken from me if I didn't control knowledge of it properly. The big fish eat the little fish, and I wasn't even a minnow. I trusted the doctors at CytoTek, but only so far. Even Dr. Pensall.

But who was I kidding? I didn't tell anyone. Not my mother, not Ian or Gina—not even Callie.

Far worse than killing the rats was watching them revive. For hours they'd lie without moving, paws curled up, mouths open, bright pink eyes empty of life. Then, finally, the miracle would happen. A tail would twitch. Or a toe, or whisker. Soon the whole body was racked with shivers as life coursed back through every nerve and neuron.

Some of the rats thrashed wildly, breaking toes or bloodying their snouts against the wire cage. Others trembled so violently that they seemed almost to levitate, legs and tails splayed out rigidly, tongues extended as they gasped with the effort.

At long last the shaking would subside, and the rats would fall into a deep sleep that typically lasted for another several hours. When they awoke, they were whole again.

As many times as I witnessed it, I was never anything but repulsed.

The revived rats were unnatural—outside of nature. And while there may not be good or evil in nature, there may yet be good and evil in the *un*natural. There was something monstrous about them. They didn't look like other rats. They didn't behave like other rats.

It was hard to say how. I couldn't have measured it in scientifically sound units. But somehow I knew it was true.

And they grew sick as the weeks wore on. Their behavior became erratic. It began as listlessness, then turned into an unpredictable hostility. I started wearing heavy gloves when I handled them—something I'd never done before—after I was bitten for the third time.

And yet I couldn't help but go forward with my experiment.

I jerked the steering wheel toward Callie as

the Triumph fishtailed to the right, my thoughts snapping back to the present. The road was really getting bad now. The sleet was coming down hard, and branches heavy with ice hung down and thwacked against the windshield.

"Almost there," Callie whispered.

We emerged into the same field we'd seen last Halloween. Now, illumined by the Triumph's headlights, it lay eerily white and ghostly in the falling sleet.

"Now what?" I asked.

"Now we go inside," she said. "Grab the presents and let's go."

We raced head-down over the slippery grass and up onto the porch of the old farmhouse.

"While you've been hard at work in your lab"—Callie shot me a glance—"I've been working too." She stamped the ice off her shoes. "Merry Christmas, Alec," she said, opening the front door.

Inside was a crackling fire in the fireplace. There was a table set in the middle of the room, complete with white tablecloth and lit candle stuck in an empty wine bottle. Two chairs next to the table, along with a bottle of champagne resting in a bucket of ice. On the table were two champagne glasses.

The room had been cleared of all the other junk and debris and, at least in the low light of the fireplace and candles, looked quite tidy. Even clean.

"Callie, this is amazing."

"Nothing much, really. Just a little sweeping up. And my folks will never even know I borrowed the tablecloth, candles, and glasses. Everything else came from right here—except the champagne, of course. Hopefully the 'rents won't notice I borrowed *that*."

"Well, what can I say but—merry Christmas and let's crack open the booze."

"Yes, let's," she said, taking her seat at the table while I untwisted the wire on the champagne and eased the cork out with my thumbs. "Now you know why I was in such a hurry to get over here—before the candle and the fire in the fireplace burned down, and the ice in the bucket melted."

"You can rush me"—*pop!*—"anytime." I filled our glasses.

"Here's to Alec and Callie," she said.

"To us."

We unwrapped our presents. As I'd hoped, Callie loved the photo collage I'd made for her.

Callie said she had made something for me, too.

It was a sweater.

"I didn't know you could knit." I pulled it on over my head. It was a solid navy-blue crewneck that clashed beautifully with the red-and-green tie underneath.

"I couldn't," said Callie. "This is my first one. My mom helped me."

"It fits perfectly," I said, patting my chest and arms. Well, that's the difference between you and me, I thought. I waited until Christmas Eve to wish wildly that I knew how to knit a sweater and had already done so, whereas you planned ahead and actually made me one. "It's beautiful."

"It's not so hard. I'll teach you."

"No, thanks. I don't think I have the patience for it."

Something was bothering me, though.

"Callie, why did you do this?"

"What?"

"You know." I gestured at the room around us. "This." The fire was burning low now, though the embers still radiated plenty of heat. Shadows danced on the walls. "Why this place, when it freaked you out so much last time you were here?"

131

"I decided I was being a baby," she said. "I felt terrible about breaking up the Halloween party you'd planned for Gina and Ian and me. It was so stupid."

"It wasn't stupid."

"Yes, it was. I let my imagination get the better of me. You were right about my—about my dreams of Jessie. It's just superstition." She waved her hand, as if brushing aside her fears. "And all the while I was here cleaning up the room, setting up the table, building the fire in the fireplace, I never felt the least bit creeped out. So there you are. I was just being silly."

"You weren't being silly." I took her hand.

"Besides," she said, brightening, "where else were we going to get some privacy?"

"Merry Christmas to us," I said as I leaned forward, my lips meeting Callie's.

Ten

◆

When I look back on my life, I suppose I'd pick as the high point those few hours, the two of us, alone, exchanging presents, happy.

Callie.

A small, pockmarked mirror hangs from a rusty nail in the gray concrete of my cell wall. For hours on end I've stared into my own tired eyes, repeating your name over and over.

Callie, Callie.

I don't know why it makes me feel better, but it does. There's so much I don't understand. I— *I*—who discovered the secret of life, knew nothing of life at all. *Know* nothing of life. And less of death.

Though soon I'll find out more than I want to know.

We'd never made love before. That night, in your sleeping bag, on an old musty mattress, we did.

Afterward there was a growing desperation in you. I could sense it. You were scared, you were trembling, you were crying, and I didn't know why.

It was okay, I told you. I loved you.

But you kept crying, disconsolately, hysterically, tears streaming down your cheeks, puddling in the hollows of your bare collarbone, your breath coming short and tight, in choked gasps. Struggling to put on your shirt and your jeans. Hair wild, eyes darting across the room, searching for demons that neither of us could see. Gathering up your shoes, your socks, your life, and running barefoot into the night.

She was out the door before I knew what was happening.

"Callie!" I shouted after her, but she'd already disappeared into the murky darkness.

Yanking on my clothes, including the new blue sweater, as fast as I could, I took off after her, almost falling as I slipped on the first porch step. A layer of solid ice at least a quarter-inch thick glazed every surface, and the sleet was still coming down hard.

I hoped she'd at least have sense enough to go to the car, but when I got there, she wasn't inside.

Damn. Where could she have gone to?

The only thing I could do was get in the car and drive down the road, praying she'd gone that direction. If she'd headed into the forest, I'd never be able to find her . . . and I didn't want to think about that.

After several seconds of frantic chipping, I realized there was no way I was going to be able to get the ice off the Triumph's windshield, at least until the heater was going and the ice started to melt a little. So, leaning my head out the rolled-down window so I could see, I drove slowly down the slick road, sleet stinging my eyes and cheeks like hundreds of tiny needles.

There! In the road not far up ahead a crouched figure slipped and stumbled along. I beeped the horn and pulled up beside her, un-latching the passenger-side door.

"Get in!" I hollered, and she did.

She looked a mess. She'd pushed her feet into her shoes, though they were still untied.

She was wearing her socks on her hands to keep them warm. She looked like one of those bag ladies you see wandering around downtown Seattle shouting at their reflections in shop windows.

"Callie, you scared me half to death. What's the matter with you?"

"Don't yell at me," she muttered through chattering teeth. She was still crying. Her entire upper body trembled visibly from the cold.

I said nothing, poked my head back out the window, and concentrated on navigating the icy road. Our Christmas celebration was over, and I was taking her home. We drove slowly for several minutes more. Then I pulled my head back in and slowed the car to a halt.

"Damn," I said to myself.

"Why did you stop?" Callie asked. The tears and sleet that caked her face were beginning to melt in the heat of the car's interior.

"There's a tree on the road up ahead." I gestured at the opaque windshield. "There's so much ice, the tree must have fallen over with the weight."

"Drive around it, then," Callie said, her voice rising.

"Callie, I can't do that. The tree goes all the

way across the road. With all this ice, in this little car—we'd get stuck in the woods for sure. We'll have to back up to the house, where at least there's a fire to keep us warm, and wait until morning to try to get out."

"No," she said. "No. I can't go back there."

"Well, you're gonna have to." I meant it to sound jovial, to buck her up, but it came out sounding harsh.

"No!" she spat out.

"Look, Callie, we really have no ch—"

"*No! I can't go back there,*" she repeated, now shaking her head.

"Callie, you—"

"*No!*" she screamed, flinging open the door and throwing herself headfirst out onto the road. I tried to grab her, but she kicked at me and scrambled away.

The first thing I saw when I got out of the car was the silhouette of an electrical tower swimming against the milky sky. I remembered having noticed it last Halloween, when we'd all driven out to the farmhouse. Callie was running toward the tree that lay across the road. But there was something else in the road. Something moving snakelike, something whipping back and forth, jumping unpredictably, popping, cracking . . . something—

"Callie, *don't!*"

I believe she never saw the severed power line that sputtered with live electricity and struck her down.

She was lying on the icy road, the wire dancing across her body like a cobra guarding its kill.

Impulsively, recklessly, I bolted forward, grasping her wrist as the live wire, shooting deadly sparks from its end, flopped menacingly several feet away. Insane with panic, I dragged her limp body across the slippery road and back to the car.

"Callie! Callie, are you okay?"

No answer.

No response to gentle slaps on the cheek. Her eyes open, pupils dilated, seeing nothing. She was not breathing. I ripped off the socks that she was still wearing like mittens. There was no pulse. No pulse.

My world grew black, then red, then black. There was no sound. I could no longer feel the sleet striking my face or the cold on my fingers and toes. The world had ceased to be a real place.

I tried to revive her. I tried. I performed CPR upon her. Pound, pound, pound, pound upon her chest, then fill her lungs with my own strangled breath. No pulse. Pound, pound, pound, breathe. Pound, pound, breathe. Pound. Breathe. Pound. No pulse.

No pulse.

Sound came back to me. There was a scream. I was screaming. Callie was not dead, she couldn't be, she couldn't be, I couldn't let her be.

No pulse.

No pulse.

I rose. Inside the trunk of the car was a box I'd picked up from CytoTek that afternoon. In the box was a syringe and an insulated canister. In the canister was a vial. In the vial was a fluid.

The world was not a real place. I opened the trunk. I removed the box. I opened the canister. I inserted the syringe into the vial. I filled the syringe.

No pulse. I couldn't let her be dead.

I injected Callie with the reanimating solution.

Eleven

◆

"Alec, wake up, dear." My mother's voice came to me. I had been dreaming. About Callie. That she was dead. My mother's face was fuzzy. I blinked, blinked again, tried to bring her into focus.

"Where am I?"

"You're in the hospital."

"Hospital?" It came back to me. The farmhouse. The ice. The tree. The wire. It wasn't a dream. Callie. "Where's Callie? What time is it?"

"Eight A.M. Sunday. Christmas morning. You've been sleeping."

"Where's Callie?" I asked again. "Is she okay? Can I see her?"

140

My mother was biting her upper lip. Her lower lip was trembling. "I'm afraid not, dear. Callie . . ."

"I've got to see her."

"Alec, she's dead." My mother was grasping my hand. She was shaking. "Callie is dead, Alec."

"No, she can't—"

"I'm sorry."

Did I scream? I must have. An orderly held me down while a nurse gave me an injection. My mother was crying. I was screaming. I was sleepy. The injection. The injection. I had to see Callie.

I slept.

They tell me that when I drove up to the hospital the night before, I was hysterical—babbling incoherently, pleading with them to care for her, insisting that she'd be okay. They took her to the emergency room and gave me a strong sedative.

They tell me I slept.

They tell me Callie Mitchell was pronounced DOA. Dead on arrival.

How had I managed to drive us to the hospital that night? I don't even remember.

When the police took me out to the site of her death the following afternoon, I saw tire tracks leading into the woods and around the fallen tree. I'll never know how the Triumph did it.

A heavyset guy in a gray trench coat asked me some questions about what had happened. He was polite, almost nice.

The fallen wire, the burn marks on Callie's body left no question as to the cause of death. The family had requested that there be no autopsy, and that the body not be embalmed. The Mitchells didn't believe in it.

I answered the cops' questions as best I could.

I failed to mention injecting Callie with anything.

The police drove me home.

I slept.

Monday afternoon.

Pictures. Images.

There was a funeral. A casket stood at the end of a long aisle of the church. Somebody spoke, a minister, I think. Something about the mystery of God's ways. Something about eternal life in the something of the Lord.

Gina's face, blotchy with tears, Ian, grasping me around the shoulders, clutching me hard, he too crying. My mother, Callie's parents, their faces.

Was I crying? I don't remember.

Approaching the casket. It seemed to float in the air before me, suspended in space, weightless, dreamlike. And her face. Skin unearthly pale. Pearly. Eyes closed peacefully, brow clear, pale lips relaxed, expressionless, calm, beautiful. She wore a simple white gown. A sprig of baby's breath adorned her temple. Upon her chest her bleached hands were folded as if the small bouquet they held was going to take flight and flutter away.

I gazed at those hands for a long, long moment, studying them for any sign of a twitch or pulse.

It'd been over thirty-six hours now.

But she was still and cold and lifeless as marble, and I stumbled away from the casket.

Then a shouting, on my right a flailing tangle of arms and legs, and three men were holding back Mr. Mitchell, and he was screaming at me, "Murderer! Murderer!" And I saw Mrs. Mitchell, all in black, veil drawn over her face, and she was weeping, while her husband shouted, "You killed my daughter! You killed my daughter!" then mumbled over and over, frothing, "Jessie, Jessie, Jessie," and I knew the poor man had broken.

There was nothing I could do. I returned to my pew alone.

I knew what I had to do. It was past midnight. I could hear the steady breathing of my mother sleeping in the next room. I must go. I must get out of this house.

Callie's parents had left after Mr. Mitchell cracked up at the funeral. Within hours, I was told, a for-sale sign was staked in their front lawn and they were seen throwing suitcases into their car and driving off. Where will they go that memory can't follow? It was going to be a long trip.

I'd forced myself to stay with the funeral procession. We drove single-file, headlights on, from the church to Hilltop Cemetery, on a low slope east of town.

I'd peered down into the deep, dark hole into which Callie was lowered. The casket thumped hollowly as the few remaining mourners tossed handfuls of dirt onto it. I almost had to smile as I threw a clump of dirt.

See you tonight, I thought, as the gravediggers began shoveling soil into the hole. Casually I noted her neighbors.

To the left: *Magnolia Richt Saylor. 1917–1988. Devoted Wife of Edgar Saylor. Beloved Mother of Dwayne and Stuart. Forever in Our Hearts.*

To the right: *Robert Charles Meadows. 1929–1990. In Heaven There Is Joy.*

I'd been planning ahead.

And I knew what I had to do now.

Get out of the house without waking Mom. Get the shovel from the garage. Slip out the side garage door, quietly, quietly, don't let the storm door bang shut behind you. Toss the shovel into the backseat of the Triumph, then into neutral and ease down the driveway, pushing with your left foot through the open door, gravel crunching softly, that won't wake her. Almost there. Turn left down the street, coast a few more feet, turn the key, put it into gear, lights, and I was outta there.

I was certain I hadn't woken my mother. She'd never know I was gone.

The cold snap that had brought the ice storm had broken, and there was hardly a sign of the sleet that had coated everything just yesterday. The night air was almost stuffy, and I knew I'd be sweating with the heat before my work was through.

It had now been more than forty-eight hours since I'd injected Callie with the reanimating solution. In that time I'd gone over in my head a thousand times what I knew of the circumstances of Callie's death and what I'd learned from working with the rats. Estimated voltage and duration of shock. Time elapsed between death and injection. Amount of solution.

The revival rate among rats, under controlled conditions in a sterile laboratory, was only about one in two. Those rats that did come back were breathing again in less than four hours. But given Callie's far greater body mass and slower metabolism . . .

There was a chance—a slim one, but a chance—that Callie might yet revive. And if she did . . .

I had to get her out of that coffin.

And now I ask myself: Why was I driving to Hilltop Cemetery that night by myself? Why had I told no one, not even Ian, of what I had done and what I hoped would happen?

Was it because I feared success as much as hoped for it?

Did I fear for Callie's very soul?

And did I fear for my own?

Callie had no headstone yet, but I had little

trouble locating her between the devoted Mrs. Saylor and the joyous Mr. Meadows. I glanced at my watch. It was nearly one. And now, grabbing the shovel and stamping it into the unpacked dirt—to work.

Two and a half hours later I pried open the lid on her casket. The sprig of baby's breath had fallen out of her hair, and the bouquet apparently had flown away. Otherwise she looked just as she had when I'd last seen her. She had not revived.

I hauled her out of the hole and carried her to the Triumph. She bent easily at the waist when I propped her in the passenger seat. Strange. . . . Shouldn't rigor mortis have set in by now?

After reclosing the casket and dumping the dirt back into the hole, I loaded the shovel into the backseat and took off.

Ellswood's a sleepy little town. No one had seen me come or go.

I couldn't take Callie home and try to hide her from my mother. But where else could I go? There was only one place I could think of.

The Triumph bottomed out as it crested a hill, rocks and dirt banging around in the rear wheel wells. The electrical tower loomed on the horizon to the right up ahead, but I ignored it. The tree had been cleared from the road and the downed wires restrung. You'd never know a girl had been killed here two nights ago.

The Triumph roared past the spot.

I lowered Callie onto the mattress and covered her with the sleeping bag. I relit one of the candles and scooted a chair up beside her. She looked as beautiful now as she ever had, and in the golden glow of candlelight, her face and hands seemed to regain their former color.

"Callie, Callie," I murmured.

There was no response.

I sat with her all through that night. Maybe I slept. Maybe I dreamed. I believe now that I did, because I kept thinking that she had revived and taken me in her arms . . . and then I'd shake the weary confusion from my head and see that she was still lying there, grim and cold as ever.

At long last the parlor began to lighten with the sky. The birds outside were twittering loudly. Morning was coming. Soon I'd have to face the terrible knowledge that Callie was dead. Some small part of me may even have been relieved that my effort to revive her had failed. I wasn't sure I really wanted that power.

I would return her to her grave, and to her eternal rest, that night.

And then I was crying, freely this time, deep heaving gasps racking my body though my mind was clear. And the birds squawked outside as the sun came up and all life rose to meet another day. And through my tears I observed a finger twitch, as if it had been pricked with a needle. And calmly I noted an eyelid flutter; then another finger twitched. And then I was no longer crying tears of grief but tears of joy, and she uttered a small moan, and I was laughing. And she raised her hand to her forehead and said, "I'm so thirsty."

Callie was alive—again.

Twelve

◆

"Alec? Alec. *Alec*."

"Huh?"

"Please stop staring out the window and try to pay attention, okay?"

"Huh? Oh, yeah. Sorry, Ms. Kelling."

"Okay. Okay, class, let's return to page ninety-seven of the textbook."

It was Monday, January 2. Back in school. I looked out the window.

Callie was alive. Callie was alive. I'd repeated those words to myself a thousand times in the last week.

When Callie first woke up, I didn't know what to do. My first impulse was to get her to the emergency room. She was still pale and sickly looking, and of course she hadn't eaten or drunk anything in days. But something held me back. The nurses would surely have recognized us—we'd been there only two nights before— and I'd have a lot of explaining to do. Question number one would've been: What's the matter with her? And question two would've been: Why isn't she dead? And I wasn't ready to deal with question two yet.

Callie was racked with tremors during the time she was coming back. The convulsions were almost unbearable to watch. But after a couple of hours they died down, and she was fully conscious, and then she slept peacefully for several hours.

"I feel terrible, Alec," she said at last. "What happened?" She looked around the parlor. "Where am I?"

I hadn't thought about how I'd tell Callie what had happened to her. How much did she know? "You're at the old farmhouse. In the parlor."

"What am I doing here?"

"You've been sick."

"Sick? I feel like I've been away a long time."

"Away?" I asked gently. "You mean asleep?"

"No. No, not asleep. I feel like I've been . . . away somewhere. Like on a long trip."

I asked her what the last thing she remembered was.

"We . . . we were here." She looked around the parlor, then down at herself. "Why am I wearing this dress? What's going on?"

This was going to be difficult. "Uh, I'll explain everything in a minute. Just tell me what you know."

"I . . . I remember being here. We were having Christmas. It was nice." She smiled shyly. "But then I began to feel . . . bad. I wanted to leave." A cloud passed over her features. "I ran. You came after me in the car. It was cold. I remember getting into the car. There was ice all over. I couldn't see out the windshield. . . ."

"And?"

"You said the car was stuck. You said there was a tree on the road and we'd have to go back. . . ." She was looking confused now, as if she was having trouble piecing together the shards of her memory.

"What do you remember next?"

"I got out of the car . . . and . . . nothing . . . I don't remember anything. . . . I was away somewhere, but I don't remember . . . And now I'm back here. But I feel like I'm not *supposed* to be here." Suddenly she looked very much afraid.

"Callie . . ." I began. And then I told her everything, starting with what happened that night—the fallen wire, the failed CPR, the injection. I couldn't look her in the eye as I explained how I'd been killing and reviving rats for over two months. Then I told her about rushing to the hospital and her being pronounced DOA. There was no reaction on her face. I told about the funeral, retrieving her from her grave, staying up with her all night, and, finally, her reviving.

She was calm. She asked pertinent questions, waiting patiently for the answers. It was almost as if the whole fantastic story had come as no great shock to her.

I asked her if she thought we should go to the hospital.

"No!" she said quickly.

"Why not? You're weak, Callie. Your life may still be in danger."

"No, no, I'm fine. I just . . . just have to be alone for a little while."

"Shouldn't we at least call your parents? I'm sure we can track them down somehow." Though I'd left out the part about her dad

153

breaking down at the funeral, I had told her they'd moved out of their house.

"No, Alec, please. I need to be alone. I need to figure things out."

"What do you need to figure out? You're alive." I sat down beside her on the mattress and put my arms around her. Her flesh beneath my fingers felt rubbery. "You're alive."

"Exactly," she said. "I'm alive. And yesterday I was dead. You make it sound like I can go home and everything'll be hunky-dory. It's not as simple as that, Alec. You know it as well as I." She looked at me coldly, and I turned away.

Standing up, I said, "I don't understand what's the matter with you."

"What's the matter with me!" Callie burst out. "Alec, I've been dead for almost three days. Dead! *That's* what's the matter with me. I need to think about things. Now promise me you won't tell anyone I'm here," she said, reaching up and taking my hand.

"Callie . . ."

"*Promise me,*" she repeated through gritted teeth, squeezing my hand so hard it ached.

"Sure. Sure, Callie. I promise."

"Thank you, Alec." She let go my hand.

I looked down. Four small crescent moons

were gouged into my palms where she had been gripping me.

"Alec. *Alec!*" Ms. Kelling's voice snapped me back to the present. "Alec, do you mind sharing with the class what is *so* fascinating about the palm of your hand?"

"Huh? Oh, nothing, Ms. Kelling. Sorry, Ms. Kelling."

"Okay, perhaps you'd prefer to spend the rest of the period in the princi—" She broke off. I think it suddenly dawned on her that the girl who'd been killed last week was my girlfriend. "—nurse's office. You look a little tired. Okay?" She mooned at me sympathetically and her eyes welled with tears.

"That's all right. I'll try to pay attention." I smiled weakly and returned to staring out the window.

"Okay. Okay, class . . ."

That afternoon I bumped into Ian and Gina in the hallway.

"Hey, Ian," I said, mustering as much as cheerfulness as I could. "Gina."

"Hey," Ian said. "How you doin', buddy?"

"I'm all right." I forced a smile. "Chemistry's a drag, but other than that, okay."

Gina looked up at me with her big watery eyes. "It's *us*, Alec. You don't have to pretend with us."

I couldn't stand being the object of such sympathy and concern. "I'm fine. Really. Not back to normal completely, of course, but really—I'm fine." Gina's eyes gazed at me tremblingly. "No need to worry."

Not long after Homecoming, I'd explained to Ian why Callie and I had rushed off that night. I'd left out some of the gorier details, but he'd gotten the gist of it—that Hillis and Ruben had tried to hurt Callie to get at me. Ever since, he'd been itching to take them apart limb by limb.

"I still want to kill Hillis and Ruben," Ian said. "Especially now that . . . you know."

"Well, that may make you feel better, but not me," I said. It was the truth. "What's the point anymore? Just let it go."

"Alec's right, Ian," Gina said. "Beating up Hillis Milner and Ruben Shiftman won't bring Callie back."

I couldn't help shooting Gina a surprised look. Why would she use that phrase, "bring Callie back"?

"Oh, I'm so sorry, Alec!" she said quickly.

Geesh, I was becoming paranoid. She'd interpreted my look as one of pain.

Just then Hillis loped by, conspicuously ignoring us. Ian made a move to go after him, but I grabbed his arm.

"Let it go, Ian." I met his eye. "Seriously."

Ian hesitated, then relaxed. "Whatever you say."

I dropped his arm. "I say we forget about those losers."

A couple of hours later, after the final bell, I was walking to the Triumph when I noticed Hillis and Ruben at the far end of the parking lot. I considered going over to them, but what could I say? What could I do? Pick a fight? Punch *both* of them out? Even if I could, what good would it do? They deserved far worse than a beating.

They were arguing about something. Hillis was making chopping motions with his hands and wagging his head back and forth. Ruben stood with his arms crossed, feet planted widely. I could hear Hillis swearing angrily at Ruben, who occasionally took a small step toward him, who in turn immediately backed up.

". . . You don't know jack about . . . You got what you always got . . ." Hillis's words drifted over to me in bits and pieces. ". . . Man, that stuff was . . . talking about. . . ."

Ruben's steps were becoming larger and more frequent. Hillis was backpedaling quickly now. I could hear Ruben, who was shouting back at Hillis now: ". . . Rip me off with that . . . worthless junk . . . owe me sixty bucks . . ." Hillis looked pretty desperate. Although he was a good five inches taller and thirty pounds heavier than Ruben, Hillis wouldn't have a chance.

I wandered over in their direction. Though I'd decided not to mess with them myself, if they wanted to beat each other up, that was okay by me. In fact, I wouldn't miss it for the world.

Hillis was backed against a white Firebird when he suddenly took a poke at Ruben, a half-closed fist upside the head. Hillis must have been pretty desperate to take on Ruben. Maybe he knew he was going to get beat up anyway, and tried to get in the first punch.

It didn't do him any good. The punch barely grazed Ruben's ear, but Ruben went berserk. He rushed at Hillis, throwing crisp, tight combinations to the body and looping rights to the face. I started trotting leisurely toward them, to break it up or scrape Hillis off the asphalt, whichever seemed most appropriate.

Hillis, however, was not able to make it to the asphalt. Ruben had him propped up on the Firebird's hood so that he couldn't even crumple and fall to the ground. Hillis squealed and grunted sickeningly as he absorbed the blows. Bright-red blood was spurting out of his nose and onto Ruben's shoulder.

As much as I enjoyed seeing Hillis get his ass kicked, I couldn't let it go on. Reluctantly I grappled Ruben around the chest from behind, and dragged him off of Hillis, who slumped onto his knees, moaning and clutching his face and gut. Someone was going to be pretty upset when they saw the blood spattered all over their nice white Firebird.

Ruben tried to shake me loose, but I had my arms clamped around him. "Get the hell off me, Baines!" he shouted.

Hillis had gotten to his feet and was slinking off, so I released Ruben but kept myself between him and Hillis.

"What's the matter with you?" he said, trying to step around me.

"Leave him alone, Ruben." I blocked his path.

"I'm gonna kill you! I'll *kill* you!" Hillis shouted, at Ruben or me or both of us—it was hard to tell. By this time he was a safe hundred feet or so away. Waving his arms, he screamed, "Man, you're dead! You're *dead*!" and loped away.

"What a dude," Ruben muttered to himself. Then, louder, to me: "Why'd you break it up, Baines? You should've let me destroy him. I thought you'd want to see that."

"Like you said, Ruben—he's not worth the trouble. But if I were you, I'd watch my back. He's a sneaky little creep."

Ruben considered this, then said, "Yeah, right." Stripping off his bloodstained shirt, he tossed it under the Firebird. "Coach warned me about fighting," he explained, and walked off toward the gym.

Coach should have warned you about buying steroids from someone who no longer had a lab to produce them in, I thought. You're liable to get ripped off.

Thirteen

◆

Wednesday. Every day was a trial now, every hour that elapsed a further test of my stability, my will, my sanity.

It'd been over a week now since Callie revived. She still hadn't eaten much, although she was drinking water like she'd sprung a leak. Her eyes, once an incredible vibrant emerald, were sunken deep into her skull and had turned the color of a rusted penny. The flesh around them was a nightmarish green-brown. The skin of her arms was bluish-white and had the texture of waxed cucumbers.

She said her fingers and toes had begun to go numb and that she was sleeping only an hour or two each night. The parlor was chilly during the day and frigid at night, but she refused to leave it, claiming the cold didn't bother her—she liked it, in fact. She wouldn't even let me light a fire—said it might attract strangers to see smoke coming out of the chimney. The mattress on which she lay had begun to take on the rancid smell of wet fur. There was an odor of decay—of death—hanging over her.

Something had gone terribly wrong with the rats, too. I had known from the start that the revival rate was not outstanding, and that even those which did revive often did not live long. Now, however, I had to face up to a problem that I hadn't really dealt with before—the revived rats were growing increasingly unstable. Violent fights, which under normal circumstances were fairly rare among laboratory animals, broke out frequently.

One morning I found rat Twenty-seven, which had been living with Thirty and Thirty-two, torn literally to shreds in its cage. Thirty and Thirty-two looked on placidly, even innocently, though both were covered in blood. I had never seen anything in a laboratory animal remotely like this display of savagery.

I was forced to isolate the revived rats in separate cages. Some of them began displaying extremely agitated behavior—scratching at the cage wire till their paws bled, suffering sudden attacks that drove them to beat their bodies against the cages.

Science, or the scientific method, had long ago gone out the window. I was willing to try anything now. The only treatment that seemed to slow the syndrome was repeated injections of the reanimating solution. But even this treatment was only temporarily effective. Eventually the rats descended into a more and more frenzied lunacy, until finally they dropped dead of exhaustion.

There seemed to be no consistency in their rates of decline. I could find no pattern in the experimental variables—voltage applied at death, time elapsed before injection, amount of reanimating solution originally administered—that would predict how rapidly a particular rat would disintegrate. It was as if it was some factor inherent in the rat itself—an inclination toward insanity, perhaps—that determined the rate. One thing was certain, however: Eventually they all went mad.

Gina and Ian thought it was I who had gone mad. I was never available for movies or anything else, and I never had a good excuse, either. Gina thought I was torturing myself out of some kind of crazed guilt—and she was partly right, though not in the way she supposed.

Ian knew enough to give me my space. I could tell he thought I'd cracked. But he must have figured I'd weather it out sooner or later, and that there was nothing he could do for me anyway. In this last respect, at least, he was right.

I received a letter from Callie's father:

January 2
Ashville, California

Dear Alec,

I said some terrible things at her funeral, which I wish I could take back. But to outlive your children, it breaks a man's heart. Maybe you'll understand that someday and forgive me. This is what's happened to Barbara and I, though, and we will have to live with it and do the best we can.

We are living with Barbara's folks, Callie's grandparents, now in California and healing. There's a lot to heal, it's going to take a long time.

Forgive me for treating you like I did. I didn't know what I was saying. I loved Callie and I know you did too. I was a fool and I'm sorry for it.

James Mitchell

I wished I could tell the man that his daughter was still alive. But Callie wouldn't have it. I was tempted to show her the letter, let her see what kind of pain her parents were in.

But deep down I knew it would be of no use. It would only make her unhappier.

I tore up the letter and didn't tell Callie about it.

My mother too thought I had gone over the edge. I was always disappearing at night and not coming back till morning—to be with Callie, of course, though Mom had no way of knowing that.

One morning she asked me where I'd gone the night before.

"Last night?" I asked.

"Yes. I know you've been going out a lot at night. I won't say sneaking out, Alec. But I wish you'd tell me what you're doing."

I said nothing.

"I'm worried about you. You look tired."

165

"I'm fine. Fine."

"It has to do with Callie, doesn't it?" she asked. "I heard you leave the house the night she was buried. Where did you go?"

I took a breath. "I can't tell you that, Mom. I'm sorry."

She'd always given me room. I was such a straight arrow, I'd never done much of anything to make her want to lay down the law. Mom didn't know how to handle me now.

"You know I trust you," she said. "If you say you're not in any trouble, I'll believe you."

"I'm not in trouble."

"I'm sorry Callie died, Alec. You don't know how much I want to protect you from the sad things. But no matter how hard we try, these things will happen. They just do. But life goes on."

"I know that." Boy, did I know that.

"I want you to know—whatever it is you're doing at night—I understand what you're going through."

But she didn't understand. She couldn't have.

Callie was experiencing something no other person had ever gone through before. A second life. A life after death.

But it was a second life that was quickly turning into a kind of second death.

And I was going through it with her, watching it happen, powerless to make it stop. And I alone was responsible.

No, Mom didn't understand what I was going through. She had no idea how it was for me.

Callie sat up on the mattress. It was a cool, damp evening. I'd come from my after-school work at CytoTek. "It's coming back to me," she said flatly.

"What's that?" I asked. I was sitting on a chair, exhausted, looking blankly at the black trees outside.

"It's coming back," she repeated. "I'm beginning to remember what it was like."

"What what was like?" I turned to her slowly.

"You know." She ran a hand through her messy hair; her fingers got caught in a tangle, and she tugged at it absently several times before giving up and withdrawing her hand. "Death. Do you want to hear about it?" She didn't wait for me to respond before continuing.

"At first it was dark and warm. I felt a rushing against my face. Not like wind—more like someone was drawing a sheet of soft velvet across me. I was falling and falling, and there was this feeling of velvet passing over my face. But I was falling up, you know?"

I sat silently, not answering. I didn't want to hear this.

"I fell toward the sky for weeks and weeks, it seemed like. I couldn't see anything, but I knew I was passing through red—dark, dark red, almost black. It was like in a dream when you can't see something—a person—but you know they're there anyway. I knew this red was there even though I couldn't see it. Then . . . then . . ." She broke off, unable to complete her thought.

"I don't know. But it's coming back to me, Alec. I'll remember it all." She hugged herself and started to rise.

"Oh, Alec, I'm so cold," she murmured, then collapsed back to a sitting position.

Her face assumed a blank, masklike expression. She moaned, and began moving her hands back and forth in front of her body in a wavelike rhythmic manner. Her left hand was cocked in close to her chest, while her right hand traced large arcs in and out. I stood up, transfixed by the strange performance.

Her fingers too were twitching rhythmically, as if she were plucking tiny moths out of the air or opening and closing an invisible fan. The moan had turned into a low hum now. Her eyes were vacant, empty.

I realized with a start that there was a connection between her humming and the motions she made with her hands. In her delirium she was playing a harp that wasn't there.

I went over to her and took her hands in my own, wanting to break the creepy spell. No sooner had I restrained her than she lashed out, striking me with the blade of her hand in the middle of the chest and sending me sprawling across the room.

Pain shot up my sternum to my shoulders, across my ribs to my spine, and down to my gut. I was a clot of agony, my arms and legs numb from the blow. I sagged on the floor, dazed, gasping for breath and trying not to barf.

I'd had the wind knocked out of me before—a couple of times playing tackle football, once falling out of a tree and landing on my back. But they were nothing compared to this. If no ribs were broken it would be a miracle. And Callie had simply flicked at me with her open hand.

"Damn, Callie," I got out at last.

She was "playing" less rhythmically now, more spasmodically, scuffing her heels on the wooden floor and clutching periodically at the neck of her dress with her left hand.

After several minutes I approached her again, cautiously this time. Her teeth were chattering and her eyes were rolled back into her head. I touched her gently. The goose bumps on her arms felt like the pebbling on a basketball.

"Callie, we have to get you to a doctor," I said.

"No, Alec, please," she whispered. She seemed to be coming out of her delirium a little. Did she even know she'd hit me? "I'll get better. You'll see. Please don't bring anyone here."

"Callie, we have to do something."

"Promise me, Alec," she said.

"I can't, Callie. You're sick. You don't know what you're saying."

"*Alec!*" she screamed, grabbing my T-shirt with both hands and clenching it tight around my throat. I gasped as the material dug into the back of my neck. "You don't know what *you're* saying! You brought me here! Didn't I once tell you I didn't want anyone trying too hard to save my life?"

I was speechless.

"That included *you!*" she yelled. "You're responsible for this! You have to do this for me!"

I took her hands and persuaded her to let go of my shirt. She was mumbling incoherently through her chattering teeth. On the table was a box I'd brought over from CytoTek earlier in the afternoon.

For days I had known that it would come to this. Callie would never willingly go to the hospital. And I could imagine the expression on the faces of the hospital staff if I were to go alone and inform them that my dead girlfriend was in desperate need of medical attention, and could you please send an ambulance: *Yeah, sure, pal. I remember the first time I got drunk too.*

How had we come to this? She pitifully lying hour after hour on the mattress, wasting away, deteriorating horribly. I practically crazed with desperation, knowing I had to do something, knowing that whatever I did was sure to be a mistake. The room, smelling of rot and disease.

She had slipped back into a delirium now, babbling random syllables quietly to herself. Better to let her simply—

No. No, I must never think that.

I walked over to the table. Inside the box were a syringe and a vial of the reanimating solution. I filled the syringe.

"This won't hurt a bit," I said to Callie as I

quickly slid the needle into her arm and pressed the plunger.

Two hours later Callie was chatting gaily, telling me about how her mother had helped her knit the sweater I was wearing, about sleeves and collars and knit one purl two. She was almost her old self again.

But underneath that sweater my chest and ribs ached all the way around to my spine.

Callie had struck me with an almost unbelievable force. I was reminded of stories of mothers who lift cars to save their babies, bedridden old men who regain the strength of their youth in time of crisis. The human body, like the mind, was a reservoir of untapped power. I wondered if Callie's declining mental state was unleashing some latent physical potency.

And I couldn't rid my mind of the image of rat Twenty-seven, torn to shreds by the savagery of his brothers.

We're driving in the Triumph with the top down. It's a beautiful early-summer day. We just graduated from high school. Everyone said my valedictorian speech was the best they'd heard in years. It was about the responsibility of future leaders to provide for a better world. Callie cheered the loudest at the end.

We're driving along the Olympic peninsula, down Route 101, through Port Angeles, Disease, Forks. To our left the mountains rise out of the mist and float on the horizon. The air is cool and clean and the Triumph hugs the asphalt. We're not going anywhere, just driving, reveling in the freedom of the highway and no school tomorrow. The summer stretches out before us like an open road.

I lean over to kiss Callie, and she kisses me back hard. I wrap my arms around her and close my eyes. Somehow I know that the Triumph will steer itself. I'm kissing Callie, and something is not right. Her teeth are dropping into my mouth. I'm gagging on them. I open my eyes and she's staring straight through me. I try to scream but can't. I pull away, push myself away from her. Her shoulder, lifeless, rubbery, feels like a balloon filled with cold cream. Her lips pull back from toothless gums. She reaches for me, and when I throw up my hand, my fingers puncture her skin with a series of small *pops*. I am screaming now but no sound comes out, and her hands encircle my neck, and I'm screaming, and her fingers tighten their grip on my throat,

173

and now the scream comes out, it's a loud buzz, a loud, insistent buzzing. . . .

Uhh. I slapped the clock-radio alarm. The familiar posters and pennants that decorated the walls of my room came into focus in the early-morning light.

I hadn't been sleeping well lately. Under a lot of pressure. Stress.

I lay back, trying to get two more winks before the snooze alarm went off. Okay to be a few minutes late to homeroom. . . . Hearing half awake the radio news/weather/traffic. Rain this morning, clearing toward . . . lanes of I-90 closed for . . . body of Ellswood High School student found . . .

I sat bolt upright. What had the announcer said? Had I been dreaming again? Something about an Ellswood student found dead?

Callie . . .

I turned up the radio and was blasted by an annoying auto-service jingle. Maybe I *had* dreamt it. When the announcer came back on, he started talking about some congressman or senator who was accused of something or other. Probably just my imagination. I had been having strange dreams lately.

After showering, I came down to breakfast.

Mom was standing in the center of the kitchen, her attention riveted by the little portable TV on the kitchen table.

"What's up?" I asked her.

Before she could reply, a TV reporter in a blue blazer gestured over his shoulder at some cops in the background and said, "Police here at the scene have cordoned off the area and are searching for clues. They will not comment on whether there are any suspects yet." He turned to the camera. "Jim Fairleigh, in Burlington Trail State Park. Chuck?"

"Thanks, Jim." Chuck, the studio anchor, clucked disapprovingly.

I was going crazy, my mind racing a thousand miles an hour. Burlington Trail . . . the police . . . Callie. Surely it isn't . . . and yet part of me almost hoped . . .

Chuck looked his unseen audience in the eye and pronounced solemnly, "The body has been identified as that of Ruben Clifford Shiftman, a seventeen-year-old senior at Ellswood High School. And now for the weather. . . ."

Fourteen

◆

"They say he was strangled," I heard some kid say three days later as I climbed out of the Triumph in the school parking lot.

"Nah. Neck was broken," said another. "Head turned around a full three hundred sixty degrees." They were standing a couple of cars away. Still a few minutes before class started. I stopped to catch the rest of the conversation.

"Gross! Hey, got a smoke you could loan me?"

"It was like in *The Exorcist*, 'cept that chick didn't get killed. Here." A lighter flicked on.

"Thanks."

"No prob. They found a piece of his tongue in the grass near where he was lying. They think he bit it off when his neck was being twisted."

"You're sick." The kid let out a barking laugh. "How do you know all this, anyway?"

"My uncle's a cop. Said it was the goriest thing he'd seen since that guy up in Rindell got caught in a baler. 'Member that?"

"Oh, man, that was sick. I see that dude around sometimes. Wonder how he drives, with those stumps. . . ."

"Uses his teeth, I guess."

"Yeah. . . . I heard he went out for a run and never came home."

"That guy in Rindell?"

"No, stupid. Ruben. His mom finally called the cops."

"You wouldn't catch me running through that park after dark. Not after this."

"You said it. What a way to go."

"Yeah. Poor Ruben. I never liked the guy anyway, but nobody deserves that. . . . See you later."

"Yeah, and hey, thanks for the smoke."

"No problem."

Poor Ruben is right, I thought. He'd been found late Thursday night, after his mother had called the police, worried when he hadn't returned from his after-dinner run on the

Burlington Trail. She was afraid he'd tripped and broken his ankle. He could die of exposure if he stayed out all night in this weather. . . .

Two cops on motorcycles rode the trail in search of him. His body was spotted not ten feet off the trail, near a patch of wild raspberries. He'd been dead since eight that evening, the medical examiner estimated.

Ruben's death was the talk of the school. Classes had been canceled on Friday, the morning after Ruben's body was discovered. The principal felt that we needed time at home to mourn our classmate privately. On the contrary. Over the weekend the grisly rumors had multiplied through the telephone wires. By Monday everyone was eager to hash over in person what they'd heard.

The circumstances of death were becoming increasingly gruesome as the stories made the rounds, but on two subjects the gossips were at a loss: who had done it, and why.

Even the teachers were talking about nothing else. I was walking past the faculty lounge when I heard Mr. Beerman say something about how, as a psychologist, he knew how upset all the students were. Then he asked if it was true that Ruben had been found with all his clothes on inside out.

I didn't bother to stop for the answer. I'd heard enough already. And unlike everyone else, I wasn't especially interested in the circumstances of the murder.

I had more important things on my mind: I knew who'd done it, and I knew why.

Hillis Milner was wrestling with a book that was wedged diagonally into the small space at the top of his locker. He punched at it with the heel of his hand to knock it loose. After that failed, he kicked at the open locker door, cursing when it rebounded and whacked him on the wrist.

I grabbed him by the shoulder and spun him around. "You're in deep trouble, Hillis."

"What are you talking about, man? Get off me." Hillis's right eye was purple from his fight with Ruben the week before, and his lower lip was still a little swollen.

"I don't know how you did it," I said, "but I know you did."

"What are you talking about?"

"You run the Burlington Trail sometimes, don't you?"

"Yeah, so what?"

"Did you run it last Thursday night?"

"I don't know. What's it to you, man?"

"Did you happen to see Ruben on the trail that night?"

"I don't know what you're talking about." He started to turn away, but I grabbed his shoulder again.

"You know what I'm talking about."

"What, Ruben? Guy's dead, man," Hillis said.

"That's right he's dead, and you killed him. After he beat you up, you said you were going to kill him. I thought you were shooting off your mouth. But you had enough chemicals in you to waste him, didn't you? You did it, like you said you would." I poked him hard in the chest with my forefinger. "Just like you tried to kill me."

"You're nuts," Hillis said, shutting his locker. "Get away from me, you lunatic."

"I know you did it," I insisted. By this time a small crowd of students had gathered around us.

Hillis thrust his pimply face into mine. "That's right, man," he said loudly, sneering. "That's right. I killed him, like you said. And if you don't shut up about it, I'm gonna kill you, too."

Was Hillis crazy, confessing like this, threatening me in front of all these people?

"You hear that?" I turned to the kids facing us. "He killed Ruben."

"Leave him alone, Alec," somebody in the crowd said.

"Yeah, knock it off," came another voice. "It's not funny."

They didn't believe me. They didn't believe *him*. He was walking away, so I grabbed him once again. "I'm telling you, this guy killed Ruben!" I shouted.

Hillis shook free. "Get out of here, you screwball. I didn't kill anybody."

"I'm not gonna let you get away with it, Hillis. I'll tell the cops everything—how you tried to kill me, how you threatened Ruben, your steroid business. . . ."

Hillis's face no longer wore a sneer. "You're out of your freaking mind, you know that?" He lowered his voice and started walking me down the hall, away from the crowd.

"Listen, you screwball," he whispered harshly into my ear, "Ruben had plenty of enemies besides me. You think I was his only dealer?" Hillis snorted. "He was slow to pay—thought a big star like him shouldn't have to. And I'm not the only one he tried to push around, you know—he was so wigged out, he'd hit anybody. Some of these guys play a lot rougher than I do. Why do you think he came to me at all?"

181

I didn't answer.

"I figure he went too far, and somebody decided to teach him a lesson. There's no maniac running around out there. These bozos"—he motioned at the students passing by us in the halls—"are like scared rabbits. Burlington Trail is safe as ever. I'm gonna go running there tonight. Ruben was snuffed. Simple as that. But not by me," he concluded. "Now shut up and get away from me," he said, shoving me in the chest where it was still sore.

"Oomph," I grunted. The liar. I didn't believe any of this bull about Ruben having other enemies. I shoved Hillis back hard.

Then he threw a roundhouse left palm-up at me, missing by a good six inches. My fist cracked sharply on his bruised eye.

"Aagh!" he yelped, clutching the right side of his face with both hands.

I waited for him to take another swing at me, but before he could, Mr. Beerman stepped out of the crowd of students, waving his arms and hollering, "Break it up, break it up!" He hitched up his pants, then took hold of Hillis and me by the collars of our T-shirts. Hillis was still grimacing in pain.

"Milner, Baines," Mr. Beerman boomed, "I've

had about enough of you two. Come with me. The rest of you"—he glared at the backs of the rapidly dispersing students—"have somewhere else to be. Unless you want to go to Mr. Gurties's office with these jokers." He hustled us by our collars down the hall.

Mr. Gurties did not like fighting, or shoving, or arguing, or even pausing in the halls of his school. Mr. Gurties liked to run a *tight ship.* Mr. Gurties was disappointed that two such fine students would behave in such a disgraceful manner. Mr. Gurties was going to do us a favor and not record this minor infraction on our permanent records. This time. Mr. Gurties was of the opinion, however, that we needed some time to cool off. Mr. Gurties wanted us to think about our actions.

Mr. Gurties sent Hillis and me home for the day.

But instead of going home, I went to visit Callie at the farmhouse.

The room reeked with the stench of rotting flesh. The carcasses of dead animals—birds, mice, squirrels, even the matted remains of a raccoon—were arranged in a circle around the fireplace, several of them hanging from hooks on the mantel like Christmas stockings. The carcasses crawled with beetles and maggots, and fat black flies buzzed clumsily about the room, knocking headlong into walls as if drunk with blood. Sticks and dead leaves were heaped inside the fireplace, but Callie wouldn't allow me to light a fire.

Callie was always in the parlor, usually faceup on the mattress and staring blankly at the ceiling, when I came to visit her. She seldom went outside—often enough, though, to amass a sizable collection of dead animals. She explained that she took short walks around the farmhouse when she couldn't sleep at night. She couldn't—or wouldn't—say why she felt compelled to erect the shrine in the fireplace.

It was obvious that she was descending into madness, just like the laboratory rats.

Despite the reanimating solution, which I was injecting her with on a daily basis now, Callie was deteriorating rapidly. Her face had assumed a trancelike, deadened expression. When she moved her lips to speak, the skin around them crinkled as if covered with a thick layer of dried calamine lotion. Garish purple and green bruises formed on her arms and legs and faded as quickly as they appeared. A viscous yellow fluid had begun to ooze from under her fingernails, though this too cleared up at times. It was as if she was rotting from the inside out.

The reanimating solution did help a little, however. She was livelier, more energetic, within hours of each injection. But I couldn't help wondering if it wouldn't be better to let her go without it. Then she would slide lower and lower . . . and that's what compelled me to continue treating her.

I couldn't allow her to die. I had brought her back, and I had to find a way to save her.

I was still working in the lab, trying to find a combination of proteins and doses that would restore dead rats to permanent full health. And while there was still hope—even a tiny one— that it was possible, I had to keep her alive.

Callie was always on the verge of delirium when I gave her the shots. I had to be careful when injecting her—I didn't want to get smacked again. I wasn't totally certain that she even understood what I was doing. And now I wonder why I never asked her in her lucid times whether she wanted the injections or not.

Today she seemed a little stronger, especially after I administered the reanimating solution. We sat and chatted, and it was almost like old times. On Friday I had told her about Ruben Shiftman's murder. She had been pretty out of it then, and I wasn't sure how much of that conversation she would remember. But she brought it up herself.

"Do they have any idea yet who killed Ruben?" she asked.

"Who, the cops?"

"Yeah."

"Nah. Rumors are flying about how it was done, but nobody has any idea who did it. A maniac in the woods is all anyone can come up with. Except me. Not that they'd listen to me."

"You know who killed Ruben?" she asked.

"I don't know for sure, but I think Hillis did." After my "conversation" with him of the morning, I was less sure than I had been.

"Why would you think that?" she asked.

"Well, Hillis tried to kill me once. And you know he'll do just about anything. Look at that stunt he pulled at Homecoming—throwing a firebomb in a crowded stadium. And even with his lab gone, he's probably got so many chemicals in his system, he doesn't know up from down. I was there when he threatened to kill Ruben—and three days later, Ruben turns up dead. . . . I'd say those are pretty good reasons for suspecting him."

"Maybe you're right," Callie admitted. "Still, do you really think he's capable of it—I mean physically? Whoever killed Ruben must have been incredibly powerful to be able to twist his head around like that."

I paused, suddenly troubled for some reason. Callie gazed at me warmly.

"That's only a sick rumor," I said. "No one besides the cops knows how he was killed, and they're not saying anything."

"I guess. . . ."

"I know. And I'm going to make sure Hillis pays for it."

"Be careful, Alec," Callie warned. "If Hillis really did kill Ruben, he must be dangerous. And he could come after you, too, if he feels threatened. He did once before."

"Well, too late now. I confronted him this morning."

"Oh, Alec. That wasn't very smart."

"I guess not." There was a short pause.

"So what did he say?"

"Hillis? Denied it, of course." I shook my head in disgust. "Made up some garbage about other dealers being mad at Ruben. Supposedly Ruben had made lots of serious enemies— owed money, got uppity, that sort of thing.

Hillis claims he got bumped off for it."

"You don't think Hillis is telling the truth about Ruben's enemies?" she asked.

"I'm not sure now. Hillis is sneaky, but he's too spineless to be a good liar. And *he* seemed to believe it, anyway. If he didn't do it, it would figure he'd be afraid of the maniac on the loose, like everyone else. But apparently he's not. He even told me he's running on the Burlington Trail tonight."

"I guess he's pretty certain that Ruben's death wasn't random," she said.

"And speaking of that, Callie, I'm worried about you out here all by yourself." I reached over and stroked her matted hair. "What if there is some sort of maniac running around?"

"Don't worry. I'll be okay."

"But don't you think we should—"

"Alec, we've already discussed this," she said curtly. "I'm not ready yet."

Callie was going to have it her way. "I don't know what I'm going to do about Hillis," I said, returning to our earlier subject. "But I have to do something. Anything." I shrugged. "If he did kill Ruben, I can't let him get away with it."

"He's not going to get away with anything." Callie took my hands. "I think you should stay out of it, though. Let the police handle it. I don't want to see you hurt."

Here was Callie worrying about *me*.

"Thanks," I said, leaning over and kissing her gently on the lips.

We were sitting on the mattress. At times like these, when Callie was feeling better, I knew that I still loved her as much as I ever had.

"I wonder about why I came back." Callie sat humming softly to herself, braiding her hair. The sun was setting, and the parlor glowed an orange pink. "There must have been a purpose. Every living thing dies." She waved at the animals strewn around the fireplace. "And yet only I came back."

"The rats," I corrected her. "Some of my laboratory rats have been reanimated too."

"Oh yes," she said. "Yes. . . . By the way, how are they doing? Are they still okay?"

"Sure," I lied. "They're fine. I'm running some experiments on them now," I added vaguely.

"That's good." She seemed satisfied by my answer. "Alec, I can see more and more clearly what happened to me, and why. I know you never believed I knew Jessie was going to die, and you

189

probably won't believe this either—but I know there's a purpose to all this. I remember death now, Alec. I remember the whole thing. Only, the more I remember, the less I can explain it."

She sat cross-legged on the mattress. I reached up from where I was lying and rubbed the back of her neck.

"Mmm, that feels good," she said. "It's like . . . like . . . when I was dead, I was okay. Everything fit. I was plugged in. I could feel death flowing through me, and it was powerful. But then I was unplugged. Jerked out."

She paused, and I shifted uncomfortably.

Then she went on. "Death isn't such a terrible thing, Alec. I should be there now, you know."

"Don't say that." I drew my hand away from her neck.

"It's true. I should be dead. It's a fact. But I'm not, and there's got to be a reason for it. Like something was out of balance and had to be evened up."

"How do you mean?"

"Well, I filled my slot and was taken out of it. Maybe the slot still needs to be filled. Maybe someone had to die to make up for my not being dead."

"But your slot will be filled eventually, Callie, when your time comes."

"You're wrong about that, Alec. My time came and went. I was supposed to die. And now some other person has to die in my place."

"Are you thinking about Ruben?"

"Not particularly," she said, but I knew she had been. "What makes you say that?"

"Nothing. It's simply that—"

"Ruben's got nothing to do with it."

"I thought, since Ruben died, and you—"

"Ruben's death has nothing to do with me, Alec."

"Okay. Okay, fine." She was beginning to act a little strangely. The reanimating solution must have been wearing off.

"But things do have a way of evening out in the end. I know that now," she concluded.

I wanted to get going. She was always worse at night. That was when the terrors came on. I couldn't bear to watch her deteriorate after the peaceful afternoon we'd had together. And besides, I didn't like the direction this conversation had been going.

I made up some excuse about having told my mom I'd be there for dinner, and made a quick exit.

On the way home I turned over Callie's remarks about things evening out in the end. What had she meant by that? Was she saying that Ruben had deserved to die? That there was some justice in it, for what he had done to her at Homecoming? Well, maybe there was.

Instead of turning down the road to my house, I kept going straight, south toward Mount Rainier. I was too rattled to go home and make small talk with my mom. I needed some time to think. I threw the Triumph into fourth gear and buzzed down the highway.

There was something that was gnawing at me even more than Callie's theories about death, though. She had mentioned that Ruben's murderer must have been very strong to have broken his neck. And she was right. If the rumor was true, the murderer must have been extraordinarily powerful.

Trouble was, I couldn't remember ever having mentioned that particular rumor to her.

Fifteen

◆

They played that lousy car-repair jingle at the exact same time every morning. I always heard it when the snooze alarm went off. Some days it was the "country" rendition, with banjos and a singer with a fake Tennessee accent. Today it was the "hard rock" version, with screaming guitars in lame imitation of Pearl Jam:

> *If your car breaks down,*
> *Don't look all over town.*
> *You know where to stop:*
> *T.J.'s Tire and Auto Body Repair Shop.*

Aargh. I slapped down hard on the clock-radio and muttered to myself that I had to find a different station.

My mother was sitting at the kitchen table when I came in for breakfast.

"Morning," I said sleepily. The kitchen didn't smell the way it usually did in the morning. "Coffee not made yet?"

She didn't reply. She was watching the little portable TV intently. A paper napkin was twisted around the forefinger of her left hand. A pile of shredded paper was on the place mat in front of her. She was crying.

"Hey, Mom, what's wrong?"

"Those poor boys," she said, her voice cracking. "What is this world coming to?"

On TV Chuck Steadman, the morning anchor, was saying something about panic gripping the small community of Ellswood.

"What's going on?" I asked, drawing up a chair next to hers.

"A boy was found dead, Alec," she said, her voice unsteady. "Another one of your classmates."

"*What?*" Someone else dead? A throb of nausea washed over me. "Who?"

"They haven't—"

The doorbell rang. Who the hell would that be at this hour?

194

"I'll answer it," Mom said.

"No, sit down," I said, taking her forearm gently. "I'll get it."

Through the frosted-glass windows that ran up either side of the front door I could see the blobby outlines of three figures—one in gray, one in tan, one in blue.

I opened the door. "Can I help—"

The guy in blue was a uniformed cop.

"Alexander Baines?" one of the other two asked. He was a grizzled, middle-aged, heavyset man in a tan trench coat.

"Yes?"

"We'd like to have a word with you, if you don't mind," said the guy in the gray trench coat. He was also middle-aged and grizzled, though he looked familiar somehow. The uniformed cop said nothing.

"Who are you?"

"Detective Sergeant Mallory," said tan trench coat, not offering his hand to shake. He indicated his partners: "Detective Inspector Debano, Officer Gates." Gray trench coat and blue uniform nodded in turn. "May we come in?"

"Uh, sure. I guess so. Come on in." I stepped aside and the three of them clumped in, Officer Gates removing his patrolman's cap as he entered. He was a young guy, probably not more than five years older than I was. In his crisp blue uniform and shiny black boots, he seemed odd man out with those older characters in their rumpled trench coats and scuffed brown wingtips.

The three cops stood stiffly in the foyer.

"What can I do for you?" I asked them.

Mallory replied: "We'd like to ask you a few questions, Alexander."

"Alec," I corrected him.

"Alec," he repeated.

What was this all about? "Shoot," I said.

"What were you doing between eight and ten o'clock last night?"

"I was out."

"Out?" said Debano gruffly. Now I recognized him—he was one of the cops who had taken me out to the fallen tree the day after Callie died. He had been a lot more polite then.

"Driving. I was out for a drive."

Debano flipped open a notebook and scribbled a few lines. I started feeling like a criminal.

Mallory spoke next. "Where did you drive to, Alex?"

"Alec."

"Sorry. Alec, where did you drive to?"

"I don't know. Around. South, toward Issaquah. What's all this about, anyway?"

Debano stepped forward. "We have information that yesterday at school you were involved in an altercation with one Hillis . . ." He flipped through his notebook and read from it. "'Milner.'" He looked up. "Is that correct?"

"I guess so." Was I going to be arrested, as well as suspended for the day, for arguing in the halls? "So?"

It was Mallory's turn again. "So, Mr. Baines, Hillis Milner was discovered dead six hours ago. Not far from where Ruben Shiftman was murdered. Now, we also have information that you were also involved in an altercation with Ruben Shiftman several weeks ago. I'm asking you again—where were you and what were you doing last night between eight and ten?"

I was speechless. Hillis. It was Hillis they were talking about on TV earlier. Hillis dead? The nausea hit me again.

"I . . . I . . ."

"Don't say anything, Alec." My mother strode into the room and faced Detective Mallory. "What's going on here? Do you have a warrant?" she demanded.

"No, ma'am, we don't," Mallory answered.

"No need for that. We just wanted to ask your son some questions."

"Mom—" I started.

"Alec, don't say another word to these gentlemen until I call a lawyer." Then, to Mallory again, she said, "What do you mean by barging in here and questioning my son?"

"Strictly informational, ma'am," he said.

"Has he been advised of his rights?"

"Well . . ."

"Can't you see we're both upset about that poor boy's death?" she cried. "It's all over the TV. What right do you have to come into my house and treat my son this way? I have half a mind to—"

"I understand how you must feel, ma'am." Mallory was groveling now. "I have a nephew at Ellswood High myself. Fine boy, fine boy. We're all very concerned. It's shocking, really. Detective Debano, Officer Gates, and I are talking to anyone who might have any useful informa—"

"Please come back later," Mom said. "I'm sure Alec would be happy to talk to the authorities—*with a lawyer present*," she added emphatically.

"Certainly, ma'am. Sorry to be a bother." Mallory turned to me. "Nice to meet you, Alex."

"You too, Detective Morley," I said sarcastically.

Mallory, Debano, and Gates hustled out the door, which I gladly held open for them. Gates hadn't said a word the whole time. I noticed he jumped in the driver's seat of their unmarked car at the curb.

As soon as they rounded the corner at the end of the street, I ran back in the house and grabbed my jacket and keys. My mother was calling after me, wanting to know where I was going, what was that all about, was I in trouble, what was I going to do?

I shut out all her questions and headed for the Triumph.

Sixteen

◆

What *was* I going to do? I started up the Triumph and pulled into the street. I wasn't sure myself.

But everything fit now. Everything fit, horribly so—the loose ends tied together like a straitjacket around me.

If I didn't know what I was going to do, what *did* I know?

I knew that the Burlington Trail, where both Ruben and Hillis had been murdered, ran by the farmhouse where Callie was staying.

I knew Callie believed that Ruben's death was tied to her own—that he had it coming. And that Hillis had it coming too.

I knew Callie had known how Ruben had been killed, even though I'd never told her about the rumor.

I knew Callie had the strength to do it—*that* I knew from experience.

I knew that Callie knew Ruben ran the trail. I had even told her Hillis would be running it last night.

Last night. Dammit! Last night there would still have been time, time at least to prevent Hillis's death, if only I had been willing to accept what deep in my heart I knew most of all: that the girl I loved was a monster.

The image of the ripped and mangled body of rat Twenty-seven flashed continuously in my head.

I knew now that Callie had killed Ruben, had twisted his neck around till it snapped, had broken it and kept twisting till his head had turned full circle.

And now she had killed Hillis as well.

I had to go to Callie. To get her to turn herself in before the madness went any further.

But I couldn't do it alone. For months I'd been shouldering everything by myself, not confiding in anyone, keeping more secrets than I could even recall. I had kept things from Callie, lied to her, lied to my mother, to Ian and Gina. I alone knew about the reanimating solution . . . the deterioration of the rats . . . Callie. And now this. It was too much.

I glanced at my watch. Ian should be finishing breakfast about now. If anyone could come through for me, it was him. I turned onto Locust Lane and pulled up in front of his house, beeping the horn hard.

His face appeared briefly in the living-room picture window as he checked who was out front honking. Moments later he came trotting down the front walk, slipping his arms into his jacket, a notebook clamped between his teeth.

"Hey!" he hollered past the notebook. He removed it. "What're you doing here? Did you hear about Hillis?"

"Get in." I pushed open the passenger door.

"What?"

"Get in."

"Why?" He climbed in and shut the door, rubbing his hands together to ward off the cold. "Gina's gonna be here to pick me up in a minute. Do you think we'll get the day off from school?"

I shifted into first, released the clutch, and slammed on the gas.

"Hey!" Ian said. "What about Gina?"

"Shut up for a minute, will you, and let me talk." I took a breath. "There's something you gotta know. . . ."

As we drove to the farmhouse, I told Ian everything. The accidental discovery of the re-animating solution. The further experiments with the rats. Injecting Callie the night she was killed. Her reanimation. The deterioration of the rats. Callie's deterioration.

I couldn't hold my secrets down anymore; they all came up in a rush. They spilled out of my mouth like vomit. And finally I spat out the conclusion: that it was Callie who'd killed Ruben and Hillis.

Ian sat silently for a few seconds after I'd finished. "It's my conclusion," he said dryly, staring out the side window, "that you're off your rocker. This isn't funny, Alec. Hillis really was killed last night."

"I know, Ian. I'm not joking. The cops were at my house this morning."

"Cops?" He turned to me. "Why?"

"They think I did it."

"That's crazy."

"Not as crazy as the truth." I shot Ian a look.

"C'mon, Alec." He laughed nervously. "What's this all about?"

"I'm telling you. Callie *murdered* Ruben and Hillis."

"Quit fooling around." He shoved my shoulder lightly. "It's not funny."

"Ian, Callie is alive. You have to believe me." I was ready to beg him.

"You're—you're serious, aren't you?"

"Never been more serious in my life."

"Alec." Ian returned to looking out the side window. "We've been friends for a long time. A long time. I know you're hurting. Callie was a great girl. A once-in-a-lifetime girl. But she's dead now. You have to face that."

"*No!*" I slammed the steering wheel with the heel of my hand. "You don't understand. I wish she *were* . . ." But even then I couldn't say it. "Callie is alive, dammit. You'll see. I'm taking you to her now."

We pulled up to the abandoned farmhouse where I had spent so much of the last two and a half weeks. It seemed like a lifetime ago that Callie had surprised me on Christmas Eve with the champagne and candles. I cut the engine and jumped out. Ian sat in the car.

"Let's go," I said.

"Whatever you say." He looked at me pityingly and got out of the car. We walked up the steps to the farmhouse porch. I pushed open the front door and peeked inside.

No Callie.

Ian followed me into the parlor.

"Okay, can you tell me what the joke is now?" he said, looking at the animal carcasses strewn around the fireplace. "Whew, sure does stink in here. Hey, what's that?" He pointed to the photograph collage I'd made for Callie, still propped in a corner where we'd left it on Christmas Eve.

"Callie?" I yelled. "Callie!"

"Cut it out, Alec," Ian said, scuffing the bare wood floor with the sole of his shoe. "You're giving me the creeps, calling her like that."

"Callie, where are you?"

Ian groaned and flopped onto the mattress.

"Callie? it's me, Alec. I brought Ian with me today."

There was no reply except the wind's whistling through a broken windowpane and the flapping of the back door on its hinges.

The back door.

"*Callie!*" I shouted, louder this time, heading for the kitchen in the back. "Callie!"

From the front yard came a scream, a scream of pure terror. It shot through the house, piercing me to the marrow.

Once, a few years ago, I was walking through the forest and came upon a raccoon with its back leg caught in an illegal trap some jerk had set. The raccoon had been there for some time—it had gnawed the leg almost clean through. It must have thought I was coming to finish it off. It let out a wail that I will never forget—high, piercing, terrible. I took a large stone and put the poor thing out of its misery, then threw it and the trap in a pond so the trapper couldn't find them.

The scream that came from the front of the house was like that raccoon's wail—rising from a deep well of animal feeling, fear undiluted by human reason.

And I recognized the voice. It was Gina's.

Seventeen

◆

Another scream shook the air around us.

I rushed to the front of the house. Ian was already out the door. He was stopped short on the porch. "What the . . . ?" he muttered.

Gina's Escort was parked next to the Triumph. She must have arrived at Ian's house just as we were leaving and followed us here.

Gina was about thirty feet beyond the cars, near the edge of the reservoir. Between us and her stood Callie, still in the soiled white gown she had been buried in. She was advancing on Gina with small, slow steps.

"Alec! Ian!" Gina cried when she saw us.

Callie turned, fixing Ian and me with a savage glare. Her rust-colored eyes no longer looked human. But unlike Gina's screams, there was no animal quality to them. They were cold, stony. Insane. Unearthly. Evil.

"Alec," Ian murmured. "What is going on here?"

"Callie, what are you—" I started.

"I told you not to bring anyone here, Alec," she hissed. "When I saw Ian was with you, I snuck out the back and came around to the reservoir. But this little twit"—she jerked her head at Gina—"drove up and saw me. Too bad. If she hadn't, Ian would never have believed you, and our secret would have been safe."

I stepped down from the porch. "Callie, we're here to help."

"*No!*" she shouted, thrashing her hands violently. "I can't be helped. Don't you understand? I should be dead. Those feelings I had last fall, that I was going to die. They were right. I *was* supposed to die. My time here was up. And when I was killed, I was supposed to *stay dead*." She bit the words off viciously.

"Callie—" I started.

"But you brought me back. Oh, you're such a genius. Such a hero. You thought you'd beaten death. I have news for you: You only cheated it. But death plays dirty too."

"I never meant to be a hero," I said feebly, moving forward a step. "I did it for you. I love you."

"I'm not the girl you loved. Death does that to a person."

"I thought I was doing the right thing," I offered.

Callie laughed contemptuously. "I never asked to be reanimated, as you call it. In fact, I asked not to be. *You're* responsible, Alec. You alone."

"So now what?" I asked lamely. "Will you come with us?"

"You still don't get it, do you, Alec? I may be reanimated, but death is inside me. It fills me up. Overflows. And I'm going to spread it around a little."

"There's been enough dying," I pleaded with her, but I knew it was no use. Again rat Twenty-seven flashed in my mind. "Let it stop now."

"I'm afraid it doesn't work that way. Now or later, death always wins in the end."

"Oh, no," Gina cried as Callie turned to her.

"Callie, no!" I yelled. Gina was scrambling along the reservoir's bank, struggling to get her footing in the loose sand. Callie was almost on top of her.

Ian bolted past me and charged toward Callie.

It was as if I was watching this scene through the wrong end of a telescope. The three of them seemed very small and remote, and though it all happened in a fraction of a second, I remember quite clearly a number of thoughts that floated simultaneously through my head. One of them was: *I've never seen that purple blouse Gina has on before. It must be new.* Another was: *The car felt a little out of alignment on the way over. I'll have to take it over to T.J.'s and have them look at it.* And the third was: *No, Ian. Don't.*

"No, Ian!" I shouted. "Don't!"

Callie spun around as Ian reached her. She lashed out with her right fist and backhanded him across the cheekbone. There was a loud, hollow *pop,* almost like the *thwack* a golfer makes when driving the ball. Ian had been running full tilt into the blow, and he was sent sprawling through the air. He landed in a crumpled heap at the base of a small log.

"Dope," Callie said.

Gina collapsed in the sand, gasping back tears of hysteria.

Callie seemed unsure of what to do next. She scowled at me silently as I walked over to Ian.

I prayed that he hadn't been hurt too badly.

He had landed chest down. His hands lay palms-up by his sides. The toes of his shoes dug into the sand. And his eyes stared straight up at the sky, a horrible grimace contorting his face.

I realized with a surge of nausea that his head had been spun all the way around.

A fly lit on his forehead and then buzzed off.

"Ian . . ." I choked out. "You killed him, Callie."

"Don't try to stop me, Alec," Callie said. "I don't want to have to hurt you."

"Alec, help me . . ." Gina whimpered.

"'Alec, help me,'" Callie mimicked, sneering at Gina. "Help you what?"

"Alec—" Gina started, but Callie had pounced.

I knew I couldn't restrain Callie with my bare hands alone. What could I hit her with? I spotted the log Ian had fallen next to. It was six or seven feet long and about half a foot in diameter. As I bent down to grab one end of it, Gina screamed one last time.

"*Nooo!*"

She was on her hands and knees. Callie was straddling her, holding her head up by the hair with her left hand. With her right hand Callie reached around, grabbed Gina's chin, and yanked.

I squeezed my eyes shut.

When I opened them, Callie was still standing over Gina, holding her head up by the hair. Gina's eyes were closed and her jaw hung slack, but otherwise she seemed unharmed. I noticed the hair Callie gripped in her left hand was twisted oddly into a tight topknot.

Then I realized it wasn't the hair that had been twisted. It was the head underneath.

Callie let go of Gina's hair, and it resumed its flawless pageboy even before her head jerked to the left a quarter turn. After a moment Gina dropped like a sack, her new purple blouse settling silkily on the sand. Her face rested on its right cheek, and a stream of blood flowed between the rows of white teeth.

My stomach rose up into my throat and spilled out.

Her legs spread broadly in the ragged white gown, Gina's broken body between her feet, Callie stood unmoving.

I coughed the bile out of my nostrils.

My fingers dug under the log and pried it out of the sand. Callie still straddled Gina, panting softly. She wasn't watching me.

I lunged forward and swung the heavy log with both hands, clipping Callie across the shoulder and back of the head with the tip of it. She staggered several steps from the blow and then dropped to her knees, dazed.

"Callie, please," I found myself saying. "It's not too late. Come with me and we can get help."

"No, Alec. It's over now."

"Callie, please."

"No," she repeated.

"I still love you," I whispered. And despite everything, it was true.

She picked herself up and stumbled along the bank. A rivulet of milky blood ran from her left ear down her neck. Her fingers splayed with the effort of walking. She threw her feet out in front of her as if the ground were unsteady.

I held up the log and went after her.

She was sticking to the bank, slogging through the loose sand near the water. She slipped once or twice but immediately pulled herself up and kept going, where and why I didn't know.

We'd gone more than halfway around the reservoir when I realized she was heading for the pier.

The pier jutted about twenty-five feet into the center of the reservoir. Half of its planks were missing, and the ones that remained looked too rotted away to support any weight.

Callie stepped onto the first one. It held.

She moved to the next plank, and the next, and the next one after that, until she was at the very end of the pier. The sun was now high in the sky, and the dirty black water of the reservoir sparkled like asphalt reflecting oncoming headlights.

Callie turned slowly and beckoned me. "Do it, Alec. Finish me off."

"What?"

"Finish me off. Kill me. I've been wanting to be dead for weeks." Momentarily she seemed softer. Almost like her old self.

"I can't do that, Callie. I can't." But I found myself taking a tentative step onto the first plank of the pier.

"You have to."

"I can't," I said, moving forward, cradling the log for balance. "Why did you do it, Callie? Why Ruben and Hillis, and why Ian and Gina?"

"Hillis and Ruben had it coming," she said, "for Homecoming. For what they did to me—and to Jessie. They deserved what they got. And believe me, Jessie would agree." She bared her teeth in a smile. "The dead aren't as forgiving as the living would like to believe."

Callie's eyes burned, and she went on. "I swore I'd get them back, even if it took till the day I died. Well"—she chuckled lowly—"it took a little longer than that, but I got them in the end."

"What about Ian and Gina?" I asked, almost sobbing now. "What did they do?"

"Ian shouldn't have come at me like that. And as for Gina—I never liked her much anyway." The coldness was back, the insanity. "Besides, Alec. Death isn't that bad." She grinned. "Take it from one who knows. Now *do it*," she commanded.

She was only ten feet away now.

"I can't." I took another step.

"You started it, Alec. You have to end it."

Only three planks away now. I lifted the log over my right shoulder, cocking it back for the blow. Callie hung her head.

My life swam before me. Everything I knew, everything I believed in told me I could not possibly kill the one person I loved most in the world.

I saw her as I had that first day I met her in

the cafeteria, beautiful, playful, mysteriously knowing, falling in love with me and making me fall in love with her.

I couldn't kill her.

"Do it!" she screamed.

I swung the log with every ounce of strength left in me.

The log connected with her skull, and she plunged off the pier, disappearing into the black water without a sound.

Eighteen

◆

"We are not going to desecrate that poor girl's body by digging her up," Detective Sergeant Mallory said. "You're going to have to come up with a better one than that, Alex."

"Alec," I said wearily.

Mallory, Detective Inspector Debano, and I were sitting around a table in the interrogation room at the police station in Ellswood. Their trench coats were slung across the table like sleeping cats.

I was being charged, based on the overwhelming circumstantial evidence, with the murders of Ruben Shiftman, Hillis Milner, Ian Golder, and Gina Phelps.

"What I don't understand, Alec, is why you killed your friends Ian and Gina. They *were* your friends, weren't they?"

"Yeah, they were my friends."

"Then why?" the detective asked again. "Why'd you do it? Did they know you'd killed the other two? Is that why you did it? To shut them up?"

"I'm telling you, I didn't kill any of them," I repeated for perhaps the hundredth time. "Callie Mitchell did."

"There you go again." I could tell Mallory was becoming as frustrated with me as I was with him. "This cock-and-bull story about your dead girlfriend doing it. You don't really expect us to believe that, do you, Alex?"

"For the last time, it's Alec! *Ec, ec, ec*."

"Don't get smart with me, wise guy. I'll knock you from here to Kennewick." Mallory slammed his fist down hard on the table. "Now answer my question: You don't really expect me to believe this crap, do you?"

"No, I don't," I admitted. "But that doesn't make it any less the truth."

Mallory got up and started pacing around the room.

Debano kicked back in his chair and lit a

cigar. "Mind if I smoke?" he asked between puffs.

"Yeah," I said. "I do."

"Good." Debano blew a thick plume of blue smoke at the overhead light. "Because you're gonna have to get used to putting up with a lot of unpleasant things. Like prison food."

"It can't be any worse than what they serve in the school cafeteria."

"Maybe not," Debano said, "but at least the school-cafeteria workers are *ex*-cons."

Part of me was starting to like old Debano. Mallory was another matter, however.

"Look, kid," Mallory said. He was behind me now, leaning over my shoulder. He smelled of coffee and garlic. I refused to meet his eye. "It'll be a lot easier on all of us if you just tell the truth. Admit you did it. Enter a plea bargain. With any luck you'll be out before you're fifty."

"Open Callie Mitchell's coffin," I said calmly. "When you find she's not there, dredge the reservoir. You'll see I'm telling the truth."

"Alec." Debano snuffed out his cigar. "Say we dig up her grave and she's not there. And say we really do find her at the bottom of the reservoir, like you claim. So what? What does it prove?" He relit the cigar. "Nothing. All it shows is that you're sick enough to desecrate the dead as well as murder the living. Detective Mallory's right. If you admit to the killings, maybe we can cut you a deal with the judge—plead temporary insanity. Argue that the tragic death of your girlfriend put you over the edge."

Debano sniffed loudly and spat on the floor. "It's going to be worse for you if you let it go to jury. You'll be convicted—I guarantee it."

He took the cigar out of his mouth, examined it distastefully, and snuffed it out again. "Alec, there's a mob outside the station right now"—he jerked his thumb over his shoulder—"that would love to skin you alive. And a jury's just a mob of twelve."

"I'm sorry," I said. "I can't confess to something I didn't do."

Debano shrugged philosophically. He and Mallory shuffled out of the room.

The smell of cigar smoke hung in the air. The trench coats eyed me from the table. I waited for the guards to come take me back to the holding pen.

Freak, psycho, ghoul. Mass murderer. Serial killer. The Straight-A Slayer. The Ellswood Mangler. I was called them all, and worse. Had them shouted at me on my way up the steps to the courthouse. Had them chanted at me till I began to believe them myself.

I saw the headlines, read the stories in the supermarket tabloids.

"Teenage Manson Broke Necks with Bare Hands" explained in gruesome detail how I allegedly preyed on my unsuspecting classmates.

"The Valedictorian's Victims" profiled Ruben (outstanding athlete, pillar of the community) and Hillis (promising career in science tragically cut short).

What a laugh. I couldn't bear to read what they had to say about Ian and Gina.

The trial went as Detective Inspector Debano said it would. Five angry men and seven outraged women would be a fair description of the jurors. If they'd had a rope, they would've lynched me from the courtroom rafters.

Mr. Beerman testified about my many fights at school, several of which he'd broken up at great risk of personal injury. The jerk did a real star turn, elaborating grandly on how, as a psychologist, he'd long ago noticed signs of mental instability in me.

His professional opinion was that I was quite insane. You mean immune, therefore, from prosecution? No, no. Completely competent to stand trial. Just insane in the sociopathic sense—whatever that meant.

He added that he'd overheard me threaten to kill both Ruben and Hillis. He seemed quite pleased with himself as he hiked up his pants and left the stand. His testimony was bull, of course, but it didn't matter.

Mr. Gurties, the principal, testified that he'd had me pegged as a troublemaker from the start. I'd always been a boat rocker. Never had pulled my weight.

None of my teachers—including Ms. Kelling, who'd always had a bit of a crush on me—would come forward and testify on my behalf.

No one from CytoTek—not even Dr. Pensall, who'd offered to help me apply for a scholarship to Cal Tech—had a good word to say about me either. It was as if I'd never been anything but a dangerous lunatic and everyone had always known it.

I couldn't blame them, though. In their minds I was already a convicted murderer. And I'm sure the mob that formed every day on the courthouse steps, shouting for my blood, had nothing to do with their failure to stand up for me.

I had no alibi for either of the first two murders. I'd been alone at CytoTek working with the rats the night Ruben was killed, and out driving the night Hillis bought it.

Various cops and forensic experts testified about the scene at the reservoir, about how all the evidence pointed to me. After all, I admitted freely that I'd been there when Ian and Gina were killed. In fact, it was I who'd brought the cops to the reservoir in the first place.

The prosecution was able to establish:

1) Motive. Hatred, in the cases of Ruben and Hillis. Cover-up, in the cases of Ian and Gina.

2) Opportunity. No alibi for the first two. My own admitted presence during the others.

3) Means. A little shakier—was I really strong enough to snap their necks? Well, *someone* had, and it might as well be me, a healthy young man.

The murder weapon was right there in the courtroom, dangling at the ends of my wrists, for all the jurors to gawk at. My own bare hands. The hands, as the prosecutor said, of a cold-blooded killer.

Could I have presented a stronger defense? Maybe. But in my heart I knew Callie was right: I alone was responsible for those deaths. I would have to pay for them.

The only thing I told my lawyer was that I

never killed anyone who wasn't dead already. That didn't give him a lot to work with.

Debano was right. The jury was not exactly sympathetic. Since they weren't given a rope, they did the next best thing. They convicted me for the murders of Ruben Shiftman, Hillis Milner, Ian Golder, and Gina Phelps.

When the jury foreman—a nice little blue-haired lady, actually—read the verdict in a voice trembling with outrage, my mother collapsed and had to be carried from the room. She hadn't spoken to me since I'd been arrested. I believe she was convinced I'd done it. And I've seen her only once since the trial.

Justice is swift and merciless in this part of the country. That's one aspect of the pioneer spirit that's been kept alive. I was charged in mid-January. The trial started in late March. The verdict came in April.

The execution was set for June.

Afterword

─────◆─────

It's amazing what they'll allow you to bring into a prison. All they want to know is, Is it a weapon? and Will it get you high? If the answer to both of these questions is no, they'll let it in.

Guys have TVs, carpets, stereos. My neighbor two doors down has a personal computer. He let me play with it a couple of times during rec period. He's teaching himself programming. Says he's getting too old for the burglary racket—got shot at last time he was arrested. He'd like to begin a new career in computers—corporate espionage, securities scams. White-collar mischief. You're not as likely to get shot, and the prisons are nicer.

You've got to admire a man who's trying to improve himself at his age.

The day's almost over. The sun splashing in at the end of the corridor is blood red now. It must have been a sad ceremony. Ellswood High graduation, I mean.

My mom came by yesterday for the first time since the trial ended. Met me in the visitors' room. Wanted to say good-bye and God bless. Tried to make small talk. Told me that she loves me.

She was wearing a stiff blue suit and black flats. She held her purse on her lap. I didn't have much to say to her. I asked her what she was going to do. She didn't know. She supposed she would move somewhere and start over.

She's still young. I told her to take care of herself, and she replied automatically, "You too," then broke down crying.

One of the guards escorted her sobbing out of the room. When he returned, the shoulder of his olive-drab uniform was black from tears.

I wonder who gave the valedictorian address. Mom told me there would be four empty chairs set out on the football field at graduation in honor of the four murdered students. Ian Golder's chair would've been around the twenty-two-yard line, I'd guess. Hillis Milner's at the thirty-eight. Gina Phelps at the forty-three. And Ruben Shiftman's around the forty-four.

Evidently they did not feel it necessary to set out a chair in memory of Callie Mitchell, also an Ellswood senior, also dead. After all, she was the murderer's girlfriend. Besides, her family, including her gossipy aunt Doreen, moved away from town months ago. Who's left to mourn her?

I am. I'm left. And I mourn her still.

They'll be coming for me soon.

As a last meal I requested lamb chops and sweet potatoes. Not my favorite, but then I wasn't planning to eat anyway. My friend two doors down had mentioned how much he missed good old pork chops and candied yams, so I ordered the closest thing to them on the prison's special menu. I told the guards who brought the meal to give it to him. I hope he appreciated it.

I prefer to have an empty stomach for what I'll be going through tonight.

As I say, it's amazing what they'll let you bring into prison. I don't have a TV or a CD player or anything like that. No, all I have is one small white metal box. Of no value to anyone. Except me.

Inside the box is an insulated canister. Inside the canister is a vial. Inside the vial is a fluid.

"Is it poison?" the guard asked me two months ago when I carried the box through the prison gate. He was holding up the vial of liquid, eyeing it suspiciously.

"No," I answered honestly.

"Is it explosive?"

"No."

"Will it get you high?"

"No."

And that was that. Took my word for it. Waved it on through. Didn't care what it was, as long as I told him it wasn't dangerous or narcotic.

Stitched into the seam of my mattress is one syringe, swiped from the infirmary when the nurse had his back turned.

I'm scheduled to be strapped into a hard wooden chair at eleven tonight. A powerful electrical current will pass from metal straps through a conducting jellylike medium and into my body. The skin around my wrists, ankles, and head will be scorched. The electricity will continue to flow until such time as my heart stops beating.

In little more than two hours, I will be dead.

They will unstrap my body from the chair, zip me into a body bag, and take me to the city morgue, where I will await burial in a pauper's grave. I specifically ordered that my body *not* be handed over to any clumsy med students for dissection.

As far as I can ascertain, the city morgue is unguarded at night. The building is locked to keep out intruders, of course. But the dead aren't going anywhere, so, unlike a prison, the locks open from the inside.

I've made the calculations. Determined the dosage and timing. Weighed the risks and the rewards. And the consequences.

I'll be injecting myself with the remainder of the reanimating solution in about fifteen minutes.

True, the reanimating solution has never before been administered *prior* to the death of the subject.

But now I think perhaps that was why the rats inevitably failed to stabilize after revival. The time elapsed between death and injection may have caused an irreversible decay to begin. If the injection comes *first*, however . . .

Well, we'll never know till someone tries it, right?

So when that first jolt of electricity hits me, numbing my fingers and toes, rattling my arms and legs, singeing my hair and tripping my heart, I'll squeeze my eyes shut, clamp my teeth together to keep from biting my tongue, and let the sweet, sweet current flow through me, happy in the thought that it may not all be over yet.

Because what the heck. I'm the first to admit I made some mistakes, some errors in judgment. I'm willing to accept that. But doesn't everyone deserve a second chance?

About the Author

David Pierce was born in Virginia and grew up in Virginia and New Jersey. He has lived in London; Providence, Rhode Island; Iowa; and New York City. Presently he lives with his wife in a little pink house in New Orleans. His favorite movie is *The Seven Samurai*, which he has seen at least a dozen times. This is Mr. Pierce's first book.

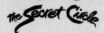